Snow Moon Dragon

Shelley Munro

Munro Press

DEDICATION

For Paul, my husband, partner in crime, and fellow adventurer.
Every day is a good day.

Note to Readers

Welcome to the world of Dragon Investigators and the taniwha. *Snow Moon Dragon*, like the other books in the series, stands alone. The story takes place in New Zealand and South Georgia, a small island in the southern Atlantic Ocean not far from Antarctica. I hope you enjoy your glimpse of both countries.

Once you finish reading *Snow Moon Dragon*, Join my newsletter (https://shelleymunro.com/newsletter/) and grab the bonus content—a deleted scene that didn't make it in the book's final version and a copy of Nyree's photo journal.

See you soon!

Shelley

Introduction

Love is a curse but also a blessing...

Dragon shifter Nyree Wirihana escapes an abusive relationship and travels to the far-flung island of South Georgia for a fresh start. No more dating for her. She's finished with men. Instead, she's content to work and explore the island while photographing the cute penguins and seals.

Dragon shifter Tāwera suffers from a curse, and for hundreds of years, he has lain in a rock pool with no hope of escape or revenge on the brother who turned him to stone.

A chance encounter changes everything, and suddenly Nyree is experiencing unique problems. Dragon problems. Romantic problems. Her peaceful man-free life becomes complicated, then danger strolls into her sanctuary and the situation becomes so much worse.

You'll enjoy this dragon romance because it contains a sexy tattooed warrior from the past plus a strong heroine who has regained her mojo and isn't afraid to kick dragon butt and face threats head-on. Sit back and enjoy the sensual sparks.

Kororāreka, Upper North Island, New Zealand, 1780

T he wind rustled the trees, playing a musical tune with the leaves. It tugged at Rāwiri's top knot as he eased into a concealed position behind a *pūriri* tree trunk. He didn't fidget, just settled, patient and careful to avoid areas where the leaf litter or a dry stick might signal his presence. The earthy scent of decaying leaves filled each steady breath, along with the crisp air foretelling rain. Moisture from the bed of ferns sank into his cloak, but he ignored the clammy coolness against his skin.

Water tinkled as it spilled over mountain rocks to the pool below. The sounds of nature worked to his advantage—a benefit since he'd misjudged his younger brother's destination. He'd mistakenly believed Tāwera when he'd told his mother he intended to visit a friend at his *whare* on the other side of the *pā*. Instead, Tāwera had ducked into the forest, walking unerringly to this private pond Rāwiri hadn't even known existed.

Now, Tāwera leaned against a tree, and his cheerful whistle carried to where Rāwiri hid. Rāwiri suspected he knew who his brother was waiting for and prayed he was wrong.

A return whistle cut through nature's music, and Tāwera straightened. Rāwiri caught the flash of eagerness as Tāwera warbled a response. An instant later, Rāwiri spied a slender form slide from the trees.

Aroha.

She ran to Tāwera, and they pressed their noses and foreheads together in the traditional *hongi*. Yet this wasn't a mere meeting of acquaintances.

This was the greeting of close friends.

Lovers.

Rāwiri wrapped his cloak tighter around frigid shoulders.

Tāwera knew Rāwiri had approached Aroha's father to arrange the joining of their families. Aroha's father had told Rāwiri he favored the match but would speak with his *whānau* and his daughter before giving his formal acceptance.

Rāwiri's chest burned, and his breaths came faster, the expulsion of air so harsh he feared discovery. For as much as he wanted to spring from concealment and rail at the couple, he clamped down his inner turmoil. Although he wished to strike his brother, now was not the time. Instead, he'd gather information and consider the problem with a cool head.

While Tāwera was the younger brother and a lesser maiden's son, he was not without *mana*. His prowess as a fearless warrior and his uncanny battle skills gave him more prestige than most. Rumor stated he had the strength of a taniwha when he sank into his battle rage. Several of the warriors swore Tāwera flew and spouted fire, but even Tāwera laughed at these tall tales and suggested the men had imbibed the *pākehā's* stinking water.

A giggle came from Aroha as Tāwera deftly untied her cloak and dropped it to the ground. Rāwiri fisted his hands, fighting the devil inside him that ordered he spring from concealment and pummel his younger brother. Luckily, prudence overrode this impulse. He sucked in a quiet breath and repeated the process to rid his body of rage and bitterness. Not the right moment to indulge his temper.

The older son of his father's first marriage, Rāwiri traced his roots back to those who'd rowed the original canoes from the homeland.

His status as the tribe's *tohunga tā moko* and his aptitude for the art of tattoo had brought him honor early in life. With his position and accumulated wealth, any father should welcome him with open arms. They should pay him for the privilege he brought to their family, the prestige that would accrue to them by association with him.

It was best he thought hard about this betrayal and consider the consequences for himself and his younger brother.

Aroha was the innocent in this situation, and it was evident to Rāwiri his younger brother considered her a prize. Tāwera had known of Rāwiri's intentions, and as the younger brother, he should've stood aside.

The couple ambled to the pool's edge and discarded their remaining clothes. Rāwiri only had eyes for Aroha—the curve of her breast and the shapely silhouette revealed in the moonlight. Uncommonly tall for a woman, she was a hard worker and always had a cheerful word for each person in the tribe, no matter their standing. Her smiles warmed many a heart. Not only was she of excellent character, but her sparkling brown eyes and lustrous black hair helped to highlight her inner beauty.

Tāwera cupped Aroha's cheek. He whispered to her, making Rāwiri's woman giggle. Rāwiri glared at Tāwera's hand, where it rested low in the small of Aroha's back. His brother urged Aroha into the water, and the pair embraced again, their bodies hidden in the shadows.

While the couple whispered and played in the water, Rāwiri forced himself to leave. He rose without haste and retreated. One thing was sure. He would take Aroha as his woman, and she would become the mother of his children. Together, they would prosper.

But Tāwera, he was a problem. His brother had acted with guile instead of honor, and he must pay for this transgression.

Rāwiri glanced both ways before he stepped onto the forest path and made haste to return to the *pā* on the hill. He called out a greeting to the warriors manning the entrance and strode to his *whare* where he currently lived alone.

Tohunga passed knowledge and experience on to their successors, and his uncle, who had lived a long life and had never taken a woman to wife, had chosen Rāwiri as his successor. Along with teaching Rāwiri tattoo skills, his uncle had passed on darker arts, which he'd made Rāwiri promise to use only as a last resort.

When Rāwiri reached his *whare*, he ducked under the low entrance decorated with beautiful and meaningful carvings he'd done himself. He crouched next to the firepit and fed the glowing embers. Although summer loomed and the *pōhutukawa* buds had burst into fiery red, a chill had sunk to Rāwiri's bones, and he needed the warmth to ease the working of his mind.

Rāwiri sank onto the woven flax mats and held his hands to the heat from the flames. The more he thought about this, the more he knew he must take a stand against his brother. Aroha was the best candidate for the mother of his children. He'd spotted her amongst the other maidens early one morning after a vivid dream had shown him the way.

Immediately, he'd known her beauty and goodness made an excellent foil for his intelligence, his skill, and cunning. They would produce beautiful offspring together, giving birth to a great legacy that would span many, many generations into the future.

For long hours, he sat and stared into the flickering flames.

Thinking.

Planning.

He considered everything his uncle Arepeta had told him during his oral teachings, twisting and turning the possibilities. He rejected some ideas and accepted parts of others.

The hour grew late, and still, Rāwiri poked at his fledgling plan. He built it piece by piece, then tore it apart and strengthened the foundations until his scheme was a thing of beauty.

Fail-safe.

Rāwiri pushed to his feet and almost fell as the blood raced back into his limbs. He rotated his hands and ankles and stepped gingerly around his *whare* interior until his strides no longer sent prickles through his legs.

He had a plan.

An audacious one, but he was of warrior stock too. In this, he was willing to take risks.

He would let the relationship play out and pretend he was a gracious loser. He'd offer his brother a unique wedding gift, and the moment his brother accepted, the fates would pivot and smile upon Rāwiri.

Once his strategy played out, he'd swoop in to console Aroha. He refused to let her slip through his fingers.

Aroha was his woman.

CHAPTER 1

Escape

Present-day, Papakura, New Zealand

T he dinner guests—a married couple and two single men—departed with smiles of thanks and waves. Nyree Wirihana stood in the doorway to her apartment and forced a return smile, despite the ticking time bomb standing at her side.

"See ya tomorrow." Ari Steele, her live-in boyfriend, bid a cheery farewell to his friends before shutting the entrance door with a decisive click.

"I'll stack the plates in the dishwasher," Nyree murmured, every instinct shouting at her to retreat and to do it now. The fresh citrus and bold amber notes of Ari's aftershave filled her nostrils, and she lengthened her steps to escape both the overpowering scent and him.

Unfortunately, Ari followed, and the fear simmering inside her ratcheted sharply upward.

"I told you I'd invited friends to dinner." Ari's tone hovered near a snarl. "You promised you'd be home in time to cook a dinner to impress." Ari's handsome face contorted into an ugly mask of fury.

Nyree took half a step back, trying to distance herself. Her breaths emerged in frantic pants. Audible gasps that signaled her panic. "I apologized."

"You went to the pub with your friends," he roared.

"We had one drink after work," she tried to explain. "One drink to celebrate getting a new client. Your friends seemed to enjoy the meal," she added, inwardly wincing. The wrong thing to say. "I'm truly sorry, Ari. The dinner slipped my mind."

"I'll give you sorry," he snarled and raised his fists.

The next day, Nyree hunched in the bus seat and waited until the other passengers stood to exit before she gritted her teeth and forced her legs to carry her weight.

Every muscle protested, and a tic in her swollen jaw jolted to life to join the painful cacophony playing through her limbs. The reek of body odor, followed by a cloud of designer perfume, had her holding her breath, and even that hurt. She bit back a distressed cry, and breathing carefully through her mouth, shuffled down the aisle. A teen girl bounded to her feet and shot into Nyree's path, jostling her without apology.

Nyree hissed, and a grunt escaped her.

The nearby passengers sent her disinterested looks, averting their gazes when they spotted her swollen jaw. The judgy whispers commenced. She'd tried to disguise the bruises and had done reasonably well, but nothing hid the swelling.

Once she'd ridden out the wave of pain, she shuffled toward the front door. The driver pulled away from the stop before she reached the exit, and tears stung her eyes.

"Wait, driver," she called.

Nyree's voice emerged at a normal register, and by a miracle, the driver—a skinny white man with a bald patch at the back of his head—heard her and slowed.

"Sorry, love," he said, glancing at her with an apology on his narrow face. "Thought everyone made it off." His expression shifted once he spotted her injuries. "Take your time."

Heat flooded her cheeks, even though kindness tinged his words. He was judging her, and the knowledge galled because he'd be right in his assumptions.

Finally, she exited the bus.

"Thank you, driver," she called.

He smiled and, with a nod, guided the bus into the flow of traffic.

Nyree hitched her handbag over her shoulder, not bracing quickly enough for the renewed flash of pain. It hit every nerve ending on the way to her ribs and chest. Once she arrived at work, she'd rest. Her receptionist job would be manageable as long as she didn't move too fast. Besides, she'd used up her sick leave. If she'd stayed home, holed up in her apartment, her sister would've blabbed to her mother about Nyree's injuries.

Her mother would sympathize and side with Ari, believing his creditable lies of illness or clumsiness as usual—if she bothered to question him. Her mother's view came from her background and life experience, while Ari had hit upon the perfect strategy to undermine Nyree in her parent's and sister's eyes.

Manipulation and charm.

Her parent would blame Nyree for not keeping a clean house and providing delicious meals. It was a small thing, she'd lecture Nyree. A tiny service for her man. When were they going to marry? Living together was a sin, and each week the church ladies asked if her daughter and her fiancé had decided on a wedding date.

Ari wanted to marry, but Nyree kept fobbing him off. Recently, he'd upped his demands to marry and start a family. This relationship was hellish. If she agreed to wed Ari, she'd set herself up for constant punishment and perhaps death, all because she wanted to hide her taniwha heritage and keep her family safe.

Ari was handsome, successful, and used his charm as a weapon to draw in the unsuspecting. She'd fallen for his gambit, his seduction smooth and practiced. Extracting herself from the relationship was so much more challenging than succumbing to him.

Not even her flurry of thoughts, her regrets, her hope for the future cut through the *thump, thump, thump* of her injuries, and it took her twice as long to walk down busy Emery Street to reach the offices of George Taniwha & Son. Once she arrived at the office building's heavy double doors, she steeled herself to pull them open. She almost cried when a stranger exited and held the door for her. Nyree nodded her thanks, and even that sent a whiplash of pain through her muscles and bones.

As a taniwha, she healed faster than most humans, but this time Ari had done a fine job. She'd go to a doctor, but imagining the pitying glances from patients and staff kept her away. A wry laugh—a tad crazed—burst free as she pictured herself in the medical waiting room. Immediately, she winced, and she rode out the darts of agony that reverberated down her body with stoicism. Yep, from experience, she'd be fine in a day or two.

Nyree entered the elevator when it arrived, thankful to travel up to their third-floor office alone. Her Uncle George and her cousin, Hone, wouldn't believe the story she intended to tell—that she'd taken a corner too fast on her bicycle. Normally, she healed overnight, or at least enough to avoid outright curiosity. She'd grown skilled at hiding injuries, but not this time.

Too bad.

Ari had made it clear their relationship was private, and she couldn't risk the consequences right now when her finances were low and escape was impossible.

The lift dinged as it reached Nyree's floor, and she dragged in a rapid breath on hearing voices coming from the reception area.

Familiar voices.

Nyree closed her eyes briefly, then straightened her shoulders. The small action sent discomfort swooping across her chest and down her torso, almost taking her out at the knees.

A groan squeezed past her clenched teeth, and the voices ceased.

"Nyree?"

An instant later, Jack Sullivan, one of her uncle's investigators, poked his head around the corner. His black brows squeezed together, and he cursed.

His wife, Emma—another investigator—appeared beside him and her blue eyes shifted to warrior-fierce.

Nyree forced herself to smile and keep walking toward them. Her cousin, Hone, appeared next, then her Uncle George and Manu Taniwha, another cousin, and the dragon in charge of the local tribe.

Manu spoke first, glaring at her with his deep brown eyes. "Who did this?"

Nyree opened her mouth to recite the lie she'd prepared before her mind came to a screeching halt. This was idiotic.

It was *crazy* to accept this as her life.

She was an intelligent woman with a job she loved and people who cared for her. Ari had been vital to her once, but each time he'd hit her, that love had died. She'd wanted to unleash her taniwha but hadn't because to do so would put her friends and family—everyone she loved—in danger.

"Nyree," Manu said, his voice deep and compelling. "I'm waiting."

Nyree inhaled and groaned at the automatic tightening of abused muscles. Lord, it hurt to breathe, to smile, to expect her body to do anything normal.

Emma stepped forward and took charge. "It's time for morning tea," she said, sweeping a lock of brown hair away from her face. "Jack, make the coffee. Manu, you can help him."

Four sets of male gazes fixed on Emma before they swung back to Nyree.

Without another word, the men dispersed, letting Emma boss them around. Her Uncle George returned to his office while the three younger men disappeared into the lunchroom. Doors clicked shut, silence fell, and Emma closed the distance between her and Nyree.

"Come and sit," Emma said, gesturing at a black leather two-seater opposite the reception desk. "Before you topple on your arse. You're shaking."

Nyree glanced down in surprise, shocked to see Emma spoke the truth. She was trembling like a leaf in a breeze. Nyree let Emma guide her to a seat.

"You sit, and I'll get us a cup of coffee. I won't be long," Emma promised.

Nyree gingerly lowered her body to the seat, another anguished groan squeezing free without her permission. Lack of sleep hadn't helped as she'd replayed the previous night. She'd been late home from work and had forgotten Ari had invited his work friends for dinner. She'd done her best with a scratch meal. During dinner, Ari had sent her chiding glances, but she'd thought she'd done well and used her initiative. She'd told Ari she'd had to work late, but he'd got it into his head that the wine he'd smelled on her when she'd walked in the door was because she'd spent time at a bar.

Not true.

Her Uncle George had poured them a glass of bubbly after they'd secured the contract from an important new client.

Her explanation hadn't appeased Ari.

As soon as their guests had left, he'd started his accusations.

When she'd told him she'd had a drink after work—one drink—he'd backhanded her. When she'd fallen, he'd kicked her twice and continued to harangue her. She'd tried to explain—she really had, but he'd decided, and that had been that. He'd morphed from Charming Ari to Monster Ari, and she'd taken the beating to protect her taniwha identity.

Again.

"Here's your coffee, Nyree. No, don't reach for it. I'll put it on the table for you."

Curvy Emma set a tray bearing two mugs of milky coffee and two pieces of shortbread on a wooden coffee table. That done, she took the seat beside Nyree.

"Thanks," Nyree said.

"No problem. I had to wrestle the guys for the shortbread, but I've been training. It was no sweat."

Nyree smiled because her cousins were quick with food. Her smile died fast since even that hurt, and Emma, bother her private-eye-attention-to-detail, noticed everything. Emma's gaze narrowed, and her mouth tightened a fraction, although her grin remained intact.

"Tell me what happened," she ordered in a deceptively pleasant tone.

Her friend practically vibrated with anger, disdain, and judgment. It was the judgment that hurt the worst. Nyree didn't understand how her relationship with Ari had drifted this far off course. To anyone else—Hana and her mother—he was charming and generous and always ready with a smile and a joke. They didn't see the danger lurking in him.

"Nyree," Emma prompted, a hard, determined edge to her verbal prod. "Don't try lying to me because I'll know."

Nyree had lied in the past, but right now, she hurt, and fatigue slowed her down. *So, so tired.* Nyree hesitated before puffing out a painful breath. "Ari has a temper. He hit me." Once the words started, they gushed forth.

"I worked late last night, and it slipped my mind Ari had guests for dinner. He was angry because I was late home and cooked an ordinary meal." Nyree shifted to ease her discomfort and winced at the jagged shard of pain that zapped down her ribs and pooled at her hips.

A gasp escaped her parted lips.

"What happened after you arrived home and realized you had guests for dinner?" Emma asked.

"Ari shouted. No, he whispered at me in a harsh voice because his guests had arrived. He'd given them drinks, and I found a bag of crisps and made a dip. As soon as I'd done that, I checked the pantry contents and prepared a pasta dish along with a garden salad and cooked an apple crumble for dessert. To finish, we had cheese and biscuits and coffee. Everyone appeared to enjoy the evening, and I was proud of myself for managing a tasty and delicious meal."

"Ari didn't agree."

Nyree winced. "No."

"You know this can't go on, right? You're a taniwha, and you should've whopped his butt."

"I couldn't tell Ari about the taniwha race." Nyree's shoulders rounded inward as her and Ari's previous night's conversation replayed through her mind. "I told Ari I wanted him to leave my apartment. That we were done." A tear escaped and ran down her cheek. Nyree jerked, and pain reverberated across her ribs and down her torso.

"He refused to leave?"

"He told me he loved me," Nyree said, her voice without tone.

Emma sniffed. "How did you feel about that?"

"I think...I think a man who loved me wouldn't keep hitting me. He wouldn't shout or threaten or treat me as insignificant. And my gut instinct wouldn't tell me never to tell him the truth about dragons."

Emma nodded. "What do you want to do?"

"I want Ari to move out, to leave me alone." But that wouldn't happen. Ari had told her as much. He'd said he loved her, but his love was a smothering blanket from which escape was impossible.

"Are you positive you can't get Ari to leave?"

"Yes." He would make her life difficult because he'd see it as a loss of *mana*. His prestige would take a hit, and their friends and family might laugh behind his back. Ari would dig in his toes and stand his ground. He'd come from a poor background and been the sole member of his family to gain a higher education. Ari's pride would plummet if she turned her back on him.

"Drink your tea," Emma ordered, her expression thoughtful. She picked up her china mug and took a sip. With a faraway gaze, Emma reached for a piece of shortbread and bit down. The cookie crunched as she nibbled. "Yum. You should have one."

"I'm not hungry," Nyree said. In truth, she hurt too much to eat. Each swallow loosed a barrage of pain because Ari had grabbed her by the neck at one stage.

Nyree closed her eyes briefly before she opened them again. Despite the pain, she forced herself to drink more of the sugary coffee Emma had poured for her. A tremor sped through her, and a few droplets of milky liquid leaped from her cup. From habit, Nyree hurriedly wiped up the splatters. Ari didn't like—

Her thoughts screeched to an appalled halt.

Ari disliked many things. Small, inconsequential things that she'd changed because they bothered him. He'd been so charming at first, and she'd been head over heels smitten with the handsome man who hailed from the North. When they met, he'd accompanied another woman, and Nyree had been at the local pub with her girlfriends. Their gazes had connected, and he'd grinned and winked at her before escorting his date from the pub. She had thought little more about him until he'd tapped her on the shoulder three weeks later at the same pub and asked if he could buy her a drink.

"I have an idea," Emma said, breaking into Nyree's wander down Memory Lane.

"If you're going to say I should go to the cops, I can't do that."

Emma drew herself up, straightening her shoulders and piercing Nyree with a direct gaze. "You should've reported him straightaway, or at least told your cousins. Men like Ari are bullies, and they prey on those who are weaker and can't fight back."

"Ari threatened to hurt my sister if I went to the cops. He'd do it too, and Hana idolizes him. She doesn't understand the face he presents to the world isn't the one he wears at home when we're alone. Mum and Hana believe Ari when he laughs and tells them I'm clumsy. He's a chameleon with his emotions."

Emma grasped Nyree's right hand and gave it a brief squeeze. "Back to my idea. I have a friend who spends the summer working in South Georgia—the island in the Atlantic, not America. South Georgia is an English territory. It's isolated, and Ari wouldn't be able to find you there. Would that interest you?"

"I've never heard of the place."

"South Georgia is near Antarctica and the Falkland Islands. Do an internet search later. The place in South Georgia where you'd be working used to be a large whaling port. Once commercial whaling ended in the sixties, they abandoned the processing plant. These days tourists and scientists conducting research visit the island."

Nyree frowned, interested despite the difficulty in escaping Ari. His threats disturbed her, and worse, he was capable of carrying out his promises. Even if she warned her mother and sister, they wouldn't believe Nyree until it was too late. Ari was that good an actor. He'd punish her family because Nyree had thwarted him. "What type of job is it?"

"A bit of everything, really. The staff greet groups of tourists and run a whaling plant tour. From the pictures I've seen, the wildlife is incredible. Lots of penguins and seals. Whales swim into the bay, now that it's illegal to hunt the creatures. Shackleton, the polar explorer, is buried in the Grytviken cemetery. They have a gift shop and a museum. Should I tell my friend you're interested?"

"What if Ari keeps his word and attacks Mum or Hana?"

"Manu and Jessalyn have a vacant property. I know they're looking for new tenants. Would it ease your mind if your mother and Hana moved in there? Manu and Jessalyn would monitor them. We will all protect them. Would you trust us to keep them safe?"

"I...I don't know," Nyree said.

Emma took the undrunk mug of coffee from Nyree's hands and set it aside. "If you don't make a change, the beatings will get worse. If you're honest with yourself, you know this. Ari might say he'll change, but he won't. I'm going to take you to my doctor and get you checked out."

"No, I'll heal fast. Tomorrow, I'll be on the way to recovery," Nyree said.

"We're going to the doctor," Emma stated. "We need to document your injuries. Once we've done that, we'll work out a plan to keep you, your mother, and your sister safe. I don't know how you hid your taniwha and didn't punch back."

Nyree opened her mouth to tell Emma it was an ingrained habit to conceal her true nature, but Manu spoke first. He rounded the corner and placed his hands on his lean hips. Power radiated from him, along with intelligence and a healthy slice of pissed. His mother, who had died under mysterious circumstances two years ago, had radiated that same vibe.

"Emma is right. She will take you to visit the tribe's doctor. Once you return, we'll discuss our next steps."

"No, I need to work. I can't lose this job," Nyree said.

Ari would truly complain then. During the heady days of their relationship, she'd agreed to Ari's proposal to have a joint account. It was only later that Nyree realized her contribution was much larger than Ari's. The money mysteriously disappeared while she went through an interrogation each time she wanted to spend her wages. She'd started hoarding cash and keeping it here at the office, out of Ari's reach.

"You're a valuable employee," George Taniwha, her boss and uncle, boomed.

Emma rolled her eyes and pulled a face. "Come out here instead of hovering like a bunch of old biddies."

Heat roared through Nyree as her boss and the rest of her workmates stepped into view. She ducked her head to conceal her burning cheeks. Everyone had listened to her confession. Knew of the depths to which she'd fallen—her stupid mistakes.

Footsteps came toward her and halted.

"Nyree." Manu's voice contained authority even though it held gentleness too. "Look at me, sweetheart."

Nyree swallowed hard, and it was an effort to lift her gaze to meet his.

"I will protect your mother and Hana. You have my promise. They can move into the house on my property, and I and the others will watch over them while you're away."

"But I—"

Manu held up a hand. "The break will do you good. It will allow you to decide your future."

"But what about my apartment?"

"I will take care of that too. Do you want to keep it?"

"Yes. It took me ages to find a place I liked."

"Emma, how long is the contract in South Georgia?"

"It's for the entire summer. November to the end of February."

"Right, I'll find a short-term tenant for you. That way, we'll get Ari out and keep your apartment available for when you're ready to return home." Manu's intense gaze dared her to argue.

"But my stuff."

"Emma and Jessalyn will pack your possessions while the rest of us take care of the heavier items. The house where your mother and Hana will live has three bedrooms. We can store most of your stuff there. Will that work for you?"

Nyree dipped her head a fraction, feeling as if a steamroller had flattened her before she could flee.

"Nyree?" Manu sounded insistent this time. "Do you want this? Now is the time to tell us to go away, and you'll cope with whatever happens on your own."

A bark of laughter emerged from her as she studied her workmates.

Emma tsked. "Nyree, you don't have to do anything, but I'll give you the truth now. If you continue with the status quo, the chances are the beatings will worsen. You've read the stories in the paper, on the telly. You've seen the work we've done with the shelter. If you don't fight back, he'll kill you."

"No, it's not that bad." Shame suffused Nyree because the only one she was fooling was herself. It was simple to read her workmates' thoughts. She sucked in a careful breath because she hated to become more of a statistic, and that's what would happen if she did nothing.

She ducked her head while her mind busily worked, tossing up the consequences and Ari's probable reaction. The advantages of getting away from here and starting over. If her mother and Hana were protected, she'd be able to focus on herself and her safety.

Nyree drew in another careful breath and gingerly straightened and lifted her head. "Thank you for this opportunity."

Emma tsked for a second time. "You're family. Of course, we'd want to help you."

"Thank you," Nyree said. "A summer job on South Georgia sounds amazing."

She surreptitiously crossed her fingers and sent a prayer skyward. *Please don't let Ari spoil this opportunity for me.*

CHAPTER 2

Mysterious Gargoyle

N yree stood out on the supply ship deck, breathing in the sea air and watching the graceful glide of an albatross. Earlier, she'd marveled at a pod of orca gliding through the waves, their upright dorsal fins distinctive and majestic. The waves slapped at the ship's hull with low to medium to very loud thumps. The sounds were familiar. Comforting. She spent every moment out on the deck, despite the wind and the chill in the air, cataloging briny scents and drinking in the ocean's stark beauty in its many moods.

The trip to South Georgia from Chile took several days, and after two long flights to Argentina and onto Chile, Nyree now savored the more relaxing style of travel aboard the supply ship. She had a cabin of her own, which suited her perfectly.

With the full moon tonight, her taniwha was on the rise and with it the sexual urges that plagued her each month. Luckily, she'd hit on a workable system for her, which included a collection of vibrators and an ample supply of batteries. She hoped that once she arrived at South Georgia, she could shift to her dragon, which would nullify her urge for sex. Her dragon nature was a double-edged sword, and she either transformed or indulged herself in copious amounts of sex. Ari had enjoyed that part, and fortunately, hadn't understood what her increased sexual urges meant.

Carolyn and Keith, the married couple she'd be working with on South Georgia, had told her they'd spot land later this morning, and she was eager to see Grytviken, the place she'd live for the summer. For the first time in months, she felt young and carefree and excited to start this adventure.

A flash of worry pulsed through her, though—concern for her parent and sister—before she pushed her anxiety away. Manu and his mate, Jessalyn, had promised they'd watch over her family, and she trusted them.

Carolyn stepped to the railing at her side, her lined face filled with excitement. "Look! Do you see the penguins?"

Nyree scanned in the direction the brunette pointed and soon spotted a large group of sleek birds gliding through the water and diving beneath the surface. They swooped up and down, graceful and a delight. Nyree looked forward to seeing the colonies of king penguins massed on land and the smaller Gentoo and the Macaronis with their golden yellow forehead crests.

"We should see land in the next half hour," Keith said, who'd joined them at the rail. His sandy blond hair ruffled in the breeze, and he narrowed his brown gaze while studying the horizon.

Nyree turned to smile at the couple she'd come to like because of their laid-back attitudes and caring natures. That they hadn't been too nosy about her situation helped. "Is there a jetty?"

Keith turned to her with a nod. "Yes, but the cruise ships must moor offshore and use their inflatables to land crew and passengers. Landing our supplies is not always easy, although there is mooring available for small yachts at one of the old docks."

"You said I'd be able to walk and get outdoors," Nyree said.

"Yes, but you must always tell one of us where you're going and note your destination in the book we keep in the community area," Keith warned.

Carolyn patted Nyree's arm. "It's not that we don't trust you or wish to restrict you, dear. It's that we have only ourselves to rely on in an emergency. Danger to one places us all in peril."

Nyree smiled, having listened to this lecture or its variation several times since they left Chile. She understood, of course. South Georgia was an isolated territory. "How many scientists will be down here?"

"Oh, they'll come and go all season," Carolyn said. "They'll be pleased to see a pretty girl like you."

Nyree pulled a face. "I'm not looking for romance or sex or anything except friendship. I split from my boyfriend earlier in the year, and I'm not ready to throw myself into the dating pool anytime soon."

Carolyn laughed, taking her face from plain to arresting. "It won't stop the men flirting with you, although some of them will have wives and girlfriends."

"After they've been out camping and doing their research studies, you can smell them coming," Keith warned, his eyes twinkling. "No sensible woman would venture too close."

"That's true," Carolyn said with another tinkling laugh. She made a waving motion in front of her upturned nose. "They pong."

"I can't wait to see the penguins. The seals, too," Nyree said. "I've been reading about Sir Ernest Shackleton and his exploits. He was an interesting man. Grytviken has so much history."

"What with Shackleton's grave and the old whaling station plus the church and museum, our little community of Grytviken has a lot going for it," Keith said. "Ah, the islands are coming into sight now."

Nyree glanced in the direction he indicated and spotted the smudge of land on the horizon. Excitement pulsed in her, and she experienced a weird surge—a sense of coming home. A release of stress. Nyree bit back a snort. Now that part was natural since she'd escaped Ari, and it was a weight off her shoulders. Her gaze remained glued to the landmass as they sailed closer.

"I might go to pack the last of our belongings," Carolyn said.

"That's my cue to help," Keith said with a wink at Nyree.

"I'm already packed," Nyree said. "I'm going to stay out here and enjoy the view."

The older couple wandered off, and Nyree caught snatches of their conversation before they walked inside. Carolyn hoped that Nyree settled fast and didn't mind the isolation, unlike their last summer helper. If only they knew. This adventure was the opportunity to reset her life and make plans. It gave her the ability to sneak away and fly over the mountains—freedom of a type she'd never experience in Papakura, the suburb where she'd lived with Ari.

Life in the city meant few opportunities to fly. Yes, this was bliss since she didn't need to keep glancing over her shoulder for Ari's looming presence or ever-ready fists.

Two hours later and on land again, Nyree picked a room for herself. It was inside a prefab building and wasn't much in the beauty stakes. There were three small bedrooms, a shared bathroom, and a lounge and kitchen area. A dingy gray carpet square covered the lounge space, and the other rooms had bare wood flooring. The furnishings were sparse and well-worn, with a mud-brown couch that sagged in the middle and two mismatched chairs that might've been comfortable when they were new. Now, they bore permanent butt imprints. She didn't care. Once she arranged her possessions, it would seem more like home.

Unpacking was a breeze, and once she'd finished, she went in search of Carolyn and Keith. She found them standing in a room full of boxes.

"Can I help with anything?" she asked.

"We have to empty every box," Keith said. "Luckily, there is no one here to tell us we must do it today."

"Set me to work," Nyree said. "I'm not afraid of a little physical labor."

"Our first job is to check and dust every museum exhibit," Carolyn said. "And make sure the public areas are tourist-ready. Don't worry. We have plenty of chores to keep ourselves busy. But first, why don't we take you to see Shackleton's grave and meet the locals?"

"Yes! I'd love that. Let me get my camera."

"You have months to take photos," Keith said. "Just wander today and enjoy the wildlife's antics."

Nyree followed Keith and Carolyn past the dilapidated whaling equipment she'd read about when she'd devoured everything written about South Georgia. Huge rust-colored vats of various sizes towered overhead. A rusty old wreck crouched, partly submerged in the water, not far from a ramshackle jetty to her right. Old anchor chains stretched toward the shoreline, holding it fixed in place. Ancient brick foundations barricaded other mystery machinery within fallen and toppling walls. Nyree gazed in wonder and acute interest, taking in the bright, white museum with its red roof and green door and window surrounds.

Seals dotted the grassy area between the machinery and shoreline. Nyree inhaled, the seal and penguin smell unique and stinky—something she'd become used to given time. A seal regarded her with round black eyes from beneath a metal pipe, and a group of king penguins scooted away, charming in their black-and-white tuxedos with the bright yellow accents at their throats.

"We keep our distance as much as possible," Keith said. "We watch but never pet them since we want the animals to maintain their wildness. The seals are curious, but they can become aggressive when they have their pups. Don't worry. That's part of your training."

Nyree grinned, not trying to hide her excitement, and picked her way past the penguins and seals, following in Keith's and Carolyn's wake. They paused often to watch the birds standing in groups on the rocky shore and the nursery of seal pups swimming and playing in a shallow stream. Nyree smiled so wide her mouth hurt. She'd never tire of watching the wildlife.

It took ten minutes to navigate the grass area, skirt the seals and tufts of tussock-like grasses, and jump the stream running to the sea before they paused at the edge of the cemetery. A white-painted fence surrounded the entire plot, presumably to keep out the wildlife.

"Shackleton's grave is at the top. You'll find Frank Wild's grave there too. His stone reads *Shackleton's right-hand man.* The other graves belong to sailors, sealers, army men, and early explorers," Keith said.

"I mentioned I'm reading about Shackleton's voyages. I also have a book about the South Georgia and South Sandwich Island group."

"Well, in that case, I won't bore you with what I've learned," Keith said. "Ask questions when you're ready. I've absorbed a lot during the years we've been coming here, but I'd hate to see your eyes glaze over."

"Thanks," Nyree said. "I'll definitely ask questions. I want to learn more about the islands."

"We'll leave you here to wander around the headstones. Carolyn and I are checking the church next. I'll leave it unlocked, so explore there too. Just remember to watch where you're walking, keep your wits about you, and you'll be fine."

"Thank you, Keith," Nyree said. "I won't be long."

Carolyn waved her away. "Take your time. We'll start work tomorrow. If you want to stretch your legs, head toward the church and take the path winding up the hill. If you keep going, you'll get views over Grytviken and the next bay. Don't go too far." Carolyn glanced at Keith.

"Why don't you make sure you're back by three at the latest? I don't mean to give you a curfew, but I'd hate you to get lost or injured or have trouble on the first day," Keith added.

"If you're sure," Nyree said. "The curfew or telling you where I'm going isn't a problem. I don't mind in the slightest. I have an excellent sense of direction, though."

"Good to hear. Our last helper was hopeless and gave me headaches," Keith muttered.

"This is a test?" Nyree asked.

"No," Carolyn said.

"Yes," Keith said at the same time.

Nyree released a hoot, a foreign sound since she'd laughed little lately, and at that moment, she was so pleased she'd bowed to Emma's pressure and left New Zealand. She checked her watch. "It's one now, so I'll be back before three. Can I walk with you to the church now? I can revisit the cemetery another time."

Half an hour later, she was thankful she'd worn her hiking boots, and she powered up an incline above the tiny church. Recently renovated, the church had white walls, and the roof and spire were slate gray. She'd had a quick peek inside the quaint wooden interior and noted the upright piano before hustling away. Her mission: to get in a taniwha flight with no one any the wiser.

She hadn't flown for months, sex with Ari and use of her vibrator keeping her dragon level and content to remain in a two-legged form. A shift to dragon and flying was always best,

34

though, and physically, with tonight's full moon, she'd reap the rewards of less taniwha angst.

As soon as the small township was out of sight, Nyree scanned the terrain. Clumps of snow still lay in patches on the surrounding hills and covered the craggy mountain peaks in the distance. To her left, a stream bubbled, the water tumbling over rocks on its downhill race to the sea. The air smelled crisp and clean with a hint of herbal green and nothing artificial to mar its purity. While she searched for a concealed spot to strip, the braying cry of an albatross serenaded her. There were no trees on the island, but a type of moss and lichen and mystery plants grew between the rocks, making the entire area look green. She'd research the plant life at the first opportunity.

Ah! That curve in the hill and fall of rocks should work. After one last scan to check she was alone, she disrobed and rolled her clothes into a neat pile.

Seconds later, she rose into the air with a *whop-whop* of wings. A black dragon—the perfect color to avoid easy detection. She swooped over the hills, flying low in case anyone spotted her, although she was safe enough here. According to Keith, most of the scientists were on the peninsula, conducting counts of the penguin population. A second group was measuring a glacier for ice melt or something to do with global warming.

Nyree glided, reveling in the freedom to indulge herself while enjoying the crisp air and snow-capped mountains. She couldn't wait to email Emma and let her know she'd arrived and to thank her for suggesting this job. On her own, Nyree would never have dared, yet this was the perfect place to heal and get past her drama with Ari. The ideal place to make plans.

Nyree continued flying until she reached the highest of the white peaks and touched down to catch her breath. Today was clear with the sun shining and miles of visibility. Her tough scales and thick hide protected her from the worst cold, but she decided she'd better keep moving. She'd hate to worry Carolyn and Keith and cause trouble or, worse, attract unwanted attention.

As she flew back to the spot where she'd left her clothes, an object glinted—a rainbow of pretty colors. Curious, Nyree glided closer and landed in a small cove.

A group of the smaller black-and-white Gentoo penguins took one look at her and scuttled for cover. Their orange feet flashed in the sun. A harem of elephant seals barked, and a bulky bull seal bristled, watchful, and determined not to give up possession of the territory. Nyree ignored the wildlife, something inside propelling her to the shining object.

She reached into a rock pool and plucked a rock from the icy water with her talon. It was a carving, but what surprised her most was the paua shell eyes and the Māori symbols on what resembled a grimacing gargoyle. Curious, she traced the whorl of a mark with her claw. Questions formed in her mind. So many questions, the first being how had the carving arrived here? This cove was a fair distance from Grytviken. The statue appeared old, the surface weathered and faintly green, as if it had lain here for years.

Nyree opened her talon to return the item to the sea but hesitated, every instinct screeching in protest. She supposed she could clean it up and investigate its origins online. Even though the carving looked faintly Māori, it probably wasn't. It was her fanciful thoughts that told her this, or perhaps a slight yearning for her home. Ari had constantly chastised her for enjoying fantasy and indulging her imagination.

He hadn't liked her reading material—fantasy and sci-fi romances. Heck, he hadn't even approved of romances set in current times. He'd informed her she was far better to improve her mind by reading current affairs and history.

Ha! Since leaving New Zealand, she'd indulged herself by reading constantly, and her e-reader was chock full of books by her favorite writers.

Once again, she lowered her talon to return the gargoyle to the rock pool.

This time, an electrical charge passed through her claw, surprising her so much, she froze.

"*Utu.*"

Nyree blinked, a harsh breath hissing from her along with a curl of smoke.

Had she heard this familiar word correctly, or was her mind playing tricks on her?

She forced her frozen limbs to move, and this time, she successfully set the gargoyle on a flat gray rock.

"*Utu.*"

The Māori word for revenge floated through her mind again, spoken in a distinctly masculine rumble.

Well, that wasn't creepy at all.

Nyree backed away from the gargoyle and prepared to take to the wing.

"*Wait.*"

Once again, she stilled and swung to stare at the gargoyle. It was an ugly creation, yet something about it, along with the weird masculine voice that spoke in her mind, compelled her to take it back to Grytviken.

"*Pleeease.*"

The voice sounded forced now and carried less aggression. It was as if he—at least Nyree had the sense it was masculine—had moved into desperation. That the communication with her was taking its toll.

"*What do you want me to do?*" she thought.

"*T-take me.*"

It was a whisper of sound, but she heard nothing more despite listening intently.

Aware of the passing time, Nyree approached the gargoyle carefully, but it didn't speak again. Instead, a sense of thanks and happiness flooded her mind. Relief.

Nyree grabbed the gargoyle and lifted into the air. It was heavy but not too hefty for her to carry in flight. She wondered what Ari might make of this strangely carved gargoyle. Declared it an ugly waste of space and tossed it into the sea? She'd clean it up and place it in her lounge—unless it started creeping her out by talking to her again.

CHAPTER 3

Hope

Nyree strode to her room without running into another person. After consideration, she left the briny-scented and faintly green gargoyle in her bathroom.

"I'll be back to clean you," she told the gargoyle. "Then, after that, I'll find you a new home."

She paused and waited for the gargoyle to reply. It said nothing, and she laughed, shaking her head at herself. After the stress of the last months, she was losing her marbles. Perhaps Ari had been right when he'd told her she was stupid and best suited to a stay-at-home mother position.

"No," Nyree snapped, mentally slapping herself for buying into

Ari's hurtful words. "I am woman. Hear me roar."

She promised herself she'd either run or go through her exercise program while playing her power ballad playlist. She was *not* the woman too frozen to act, the one too fearful of ejecting Ari from her life and striving for a future she deserved.

Her imagination had *utu* or revenge on the brain since the petty part of her wanted payback for the months of emotional damage and fear she'd faced at Ari's hands.

And that was more than enough time and thoughts wasted on Ari. Nyree washed her hands and dried them before finding Keith and Carolyn and reporting for duty.

Carolyn gave her a tour of the museum and the various exhibits featuring life—both past and present—in South Georgia. Her new boss shared the highlights and told her she'd have homework since the visitors asked questions. Nyree needed to answer them or point the tourists in the right direction to discover the information for themselves. Next was a visit to the cleaning supply room since part of her duties was to keep the public toilets clean and dust the exhibits. Hints of lemon and astringent cleaners wafted from the open door where Nyree noted buckets and mops, boxes of loo roll, and shelves filled with various bottles and tins.

"I know it's a lot, and once Rose arrives, you'll take turns. Are you interested in taking the tours around the old whaling station?"

"I'd like to learn as much as I can. Until my friend suggested I apply for the job here, I'd never heard of the South Georgia and Sandwich Islands. I enjoy learning and would love to help anywhere I can."

Carolyn beamed. "Perfect answer. Some helpers we get for the season avoid anything that smacks of too much work. Your attitude is perfect because it can be lonely here for the younger people." Her gaze was penetrating. "You're a pretty girl. The scientists will be eager to meet you."

Nyree understood Carolyn without her needing to say more. "Remember, I'm out of a nasty breakup, and the last thing I want is another man. I'm interested in the wildlife rather than the nightlife. What's next on your tour?"

"Keith is wheeling up boxes of new stock. It's my job to unpack everything and refill the gaps in our shop."

"I'd love to help," Nyree said. "I'm curious to see what type of things we sell."

"We do a brisk trade in stamps and postcards, and we sell T-shirts. Visitors like to post their letters and cards here. They can take months to get home, but no one seems to mind."

"Do we take credit cards or just cash?"

"Both, but the connection for the cards is temperamental and depends on the weather," Carolyn said.

Nyree kept busy until the sun dipped low and the shadows deepened.

"You've worked hard. Come and share dinner with us," Carolyn said.

"That sounds great. What normally happens for meals?"

"Last year, we'd eat separately for dinner, but I like to have company sometimes. The girls who worked here last year kept cereal and bread in their kitchen. Neither was particularly interested in cooking."

"Sounds perfect. I enjoy cooking," Nyree said. "I'm happy to take a turn and share meals sometimes. You and Keith need private time away from me!"

"Bless you, dear." Carolyn patted Nyree's arm. "I can tell I'll enjoy this season much more than the last."

It was late by the time Nyree returned to her prefab house, the squabble of penguins and grunt of seals accompanying her journey along with the slap of waves against the jetty. Her steps dragged, her muscles fatigued from her flight and her afternoon's work, yet despite this, happiness filled her.

A shower should aid her sleep. In the bathroom, she stripped off her clothes and reached into the shower cubicle to turn on the hot water. On impulse, she picked up the green gargoyle from the bathtub and set it on the shower tiles. The heat eased the aches in her shoulders and lower back, and she noted with satisfaction the gargoyle appeared marginally cleaner and less green once she'd finished.

Tomorrow, she'd apply her scrubbing brush and clean off the last of the embedded mud and slime. After a rapid towel down, she padded to her bedroom and slid between the sheets naked. She'd save her nightwear for when she had to share the house with her fellow workers or female scientists who visited during summer.

Nyree issued a happy sigh. This was how life should be—hard work and the satisfaction of a job well done.

Friendship without fear and the acquisition of knowledge and experiences.

Freedom.

The start of a new life without fear and trouble.

Tāwera sat inside the tiny room where the woman had left him. He stared in the only direction available to him—forward—peering through the transparent wall, which was clear apart from the water droplets studding its surface. Acute shock had his mind spinning.

The dragon had responded to him.

A woman.

No one had reacted to him before, no matter how hard he'd tried to communicate.

It had been a brief window where he'd been able to focus on sending her his thoughts, and he'd ended up with a hell of a headache, but still—this was a tremendous victory.

She'd carried him to this settlement and brought him into the interior of a building. This unknown world comprised strange things he'd never encountered before, and he wished to investigate the marvels that both astounded and left him stunned. The water that had poured out on command and still dribbled on his head. *Drip. Drip. Drip.* Hot water that warmed him through and chased the chill from his bones.

Then there was the dragon-woman. She might be a taniwha since her skin, while in a two-legged form, was a honey-brown like his. Her hair was long and black like her sooty dragon, and her eyes were a golden brown.

A taniwha from his home country of *Aotearoa*, New Zealand.

A flutter started in his belly and spread outward until his entire body tingled. Hope, he realized. That he might touch and speak and smell the world around him again.

While the black dragon had been sleek and elegant, even a fraction haughty, the woman was slender as the Māori maidens of his youth. That was where the similarities ended because the clothes she wore were those of the European arrivals. Even stranger, she wore attire more suitable for a male, which left nothing to the imagination. In contrast, her underclothes were unusual and revealed rather than concealed. She'd seemed comfortable with her nakedness, unlike the prudish white women who'd sneered at him and his friends when they'd spotted them in town. Those ladies had wrinkled their noses at his flax *piupiu* and feather cloak and whisked up their skirts as if an accidental touch might harm them.

He wished he knew this woman's name and more about her. Could he trust her for one? Would she help him further now that she had removed him from the distant cove where he'd spent countless years? Was communication with her possible again?

He'd tried while she was washing, but she'd ignored his pleas for aid.

For hundreds of years, the stone had trapped him. He'd prayed for help. Railed and cried, yet until the dragon's appearance, nothing had worked.

He'd never communicated with anyone else.

The only difference was the dragon. Was that the answer? It was possible to transmit messages from taniwha to taniwha, but not while the curse kept him a prisoner, and she was in her two-legged form?

He'd need to exercise patience. Experiment. Listen and learn to understand where he was and how to return home. He eagerly anticipated confronting his brother and accusing him to his face.

He'd never imagined a family member acting with such treachery.

A soft curse escaped him, and it seemed to echo, rebounding back to him.

Patience.

After all this time, waiting should be second nature, but he found himself restive and eager to see more of the woman who had spoken with him like a friend. His savior.

If only he could escape this rock prison...

A vision of his brother's face when Tāwera challenged him had kept him sane during the endless years.

Revenge would be his, and he felt confident the woman's curiosity and kindness in rescuing him from the sea was the impetus for the start of his journey to *utu*.

CHAPTER 4

Moonlust Strikes

With each passing day, Tāwera's fascination with the lovely woman increased. His curiosity. His desperation to communicate with her. He stared out of the window into the early morning darkness, thinking, planning. *Hoping.*

The woman had scrubbed the salt, the sea, the stinky green plant off his outer shell, and he'd slowly dried. Then, she'd moved him from the small room in which water poured from the wall. His new position offered him a view of the sea and the upright black-and-white birds that waddled to and from the water. He recognized their clicks and honks and brays, but until the woman had found him, he hadn't seen the creature that made these sounds.

This change brought new brightness to his world, and he savored his enhanced senses. Even better, the woman spoke, telling Tāwera about her day. Small, inconsequential happenings, some of which mystified him. The lack of communication, however, frustrated him. He'd tried to send his thoughts over and over and over, but they never reached her.

The woman exited her sleeping room, dressed in a soft green garment that bared her long legs, and humming softly. From his position by the window, he couldn't see her, but he'd learned her routine. She'd eat and prepare for her day, then dress in the strange outdoor clothes that made her resemble a man and leave. Sometimes, she returned for nourishment, while at other times, she stayed away for long hours while he amused himself watching the creatures coming and going from the beach.

"Huh," she said, capturing his attention. "An email at long last. I'd wondered if Mum and Hana had forgotten me."

Once again, her words mystified him, but he listened closely, enjoying her soft voice and the way it caressed his mind and calmed his angst.

"I'll read it to you."

Yes, he'd enjoy hearing more of her strange world, and he wished she'd stand in front of him so he could admire her beautiful body and study her strange, sometimes scanty clothing. Warmth crept through him, and Tāwera welcomed the sensation because it meant he wasn't entirely crazy.

"'Dear Nyree, Hana and I are happy living in our new home. Manu and Jessalyn have made us welcome, and because the land is private, we enjoy the solitude, especially during the full moon. Ari came to see me at my job.'" Nyree paused, her voice cracking. She stalked into his range of vision, pale and perturbed.

Tāwera had already overheard her angry mutters about this Ari-man. They'd been together, but something terrible had happened. Nyree had left her home to escape. In the days since she'd found Tāwera and brought him here, she'd lost the tension in her shoulders. She'd relaxed and laughed more readily. She walked with a spring to her step, her hips rocking enticingly.

Now, the tension returned. Her smile vanished into a pinched line. Tāwera wished to ease her stress, and frustration assailed him at his lack of agency. A strange cracking pounded in his ears, and Tāwera feared his heart had fractured. He stretched outward, shifting within the confines of his prison. This woman had changed his drudgery to a more exciting life, even if he still struggled with his curse.

Nyree—he assumed that was her name from various conversations he'd heard—cleared her throat in a loud swallow. "I don't know what Ari's plan is, but I hate him visiting Mum or Hana. H-he'll hurt them to get to me. They can't see past his charm." She paced the length of the room and back, her cheeks rounds of red and her hands fisted. "Mum and Hana think I'm an idiot for leaving him. They don't understand."

She stomped out of his sight and back, her limbs jerking, her hands yanking at her hair. She bumped into a table and righted the cup she almost knocked to the floor.

"He's a monster. If he doesn't get his way, his charm falls by the wayside. His temper takes control. Now I've pricked his pride by leaving, he won't hesitate to strike against them."

"He hit you?"

Nyree jolted, her eyes widening. She stared at him or rather his rock prison, and a frown formed on her sun-kissed forehead. "D-did you say something?"

"This man struck you in anger?" To Tāwera's disappointment, the words didn't emerge with clarity, and when her expression remained impassive, his aggravation grew. His beleaguered heart shrank inward until the tight pressure had him wanting to roar his frustration, his disappointment.

What did he do to change his fate, to communicate with this intriguing woman?

She inched closer and ran a hand over his stone. He sighed at the gentle caress, and the force on his chest reduced, allowing him to take a full breath. Her eyes widened. "You've got a fracture. Maybe I shouldn't have let you dry out."

A crack? His rock prison had never suffered damage, not even when the sailor had dropped him into the sea. It had been the last time he'd seen the sailor.

Her finger gently traced an area on his front, and warmth emanated from her stroke.

"George, you're such an ugly gargoyle. I wonder how you ended up in the sea. The internet told me nothing, but you intrigue me."

Yes, she fascinated him too. Why did she call him George? Her taniwha status raised so many questions. Before his brother had cursed him to this endless existence, the taniwha numbers had been few. He'd never sought others, had never sensed others in his region. His mother had taught him to keep their nature a secret. She hadn't wanted him to endure the persecution her parents had suffered when all they'd craved was a peaceful existence.

Nyree stepped away from him and returned to her letter.

"'Ari told me he'd take you back if you apologized.'" Nyree scoffed, disgust ringing out in her derision. "He's a two-faced monster. He's worse than me, and I'm the taniwha."

Tāwera bade her continue because the more she spoke, the more he learned of this strange world.

"'Ari mentioned a misunderstanding. He loves you and wants a future. Children. Family. Grandchildren. There were tears in his eyes when he mentioned how much he misses you. He said he'd gone to George Taniwha & Son to ask after you, and your cousin, Hone, manhandled him from the premises. They refused to tell him anything, so he approached me. Before we discussed the matter fully, Manu arrived and forced Ari to leave. Ari begged me to call him.'" Nyree paused and made the expression of a Māori

52

warrior about to head into battle. "What a load of rubbish," she spat. "Ari is a liar, and he's trying to fool Mum. Perhaps I should've told her more instead of hiding the truth from her and Hana."

She halted and ceased her muttering, much to Tāwera's disgust. He wanted details.

This Ari-man sounded brutal. Tāwera had known some in his time—men who'd mistreated their wives. These warriors had cowered at the rear like sniveling children during a battle. They were cowards attempting to make themselves appear brave and robust by hurting those weaker.

Nyree gathered her belongings and turned off the machine she read from, as was her habit. She retreated, leaving Tāwera alone and frustrated. He ached to speak with her. A shudder rolled over him as he recalled her caress.

Most, he wanted to touch her and rid her of this terrifying Ari-man, even though she was a powerful taniwha. Why she didn't attack the man and remove the trouble he brought to her life? Was this man a taniwha too?

Perhaps the taniwha had grown into a powerful tribe during his absence.

Tāwera didn't know, and his vexation at his lack of conversation grew each day. The occasional thought reached her, but the transmission was inconsistent.

Nyree strode from the bedroom, now dressed in a formfitting shirt and leg coverings. As usual, she'd arranged her straight black hair in a braid, and it hung down her back, bouncing with each rapid step.

"Okay, George. I'm off now." She flashed a grin and hustled from the room. Seconds later, the door slammed, and he was alone.

George. Again. One of the many Nyree puzzles that plagued him.

His chest tightened again, this time in dissatisfaction—how he craved the ability to communicate aloud. Since she'd rescued him from the sea, he'd become used to hearing her speak the English language. Rāwiri and other senior members of Tāwera's tribe had declared him stupid to learn the *pākehā* words, but he enjoyed new challenges. Now, he was glad of his skill since she didn't speak Māori, despite her obvious—at least to him—heritage.

Tāwera sighed. Perhaps this was another test of his mettle, and he'd never speak with Nyree man to woman. Despondency nipped at him, and he focused on the view outside the window. He had the birds to occupy his mind, which was more than he'd had before.

Without warning, a familiar prickling started in his chest, the old awareness taking him by surprise. *The moon.* It was approaching its full cycle. Another week before it waned again.

If he'd been in his two-legged state, he'd have shifted to a dragon and gone for a long flight, or when he and Aroha were together, he'd make love to appease his taniwha and maintain his control. He had no idea why this recognition was occurring now when his taniwha had remained inert since the curse had entrapped him. It had to be the woman's presence.

Ah, so many questions and not a single answer.

"What are we doing today?" Nyree asked Carolyn.

"How about dusting the next museum exhibits on the list? We have a cruise ship arriving at eleven. I'll get you to cover the shop today, and I'll do the whaling station tour."

"Righto. I'll start the dusting now." Nyree collected the basket of cleaning materials from the storage cupboard and set to work. A tingling awareness of the moon prickled in her chest. It was full in three nights. Tonight, she'd sneak out and fly.

Given her frustration, she'd need to use her vibrator too. *Weird.* Typically, her almost daily flights would nullify the edginess of moonlust.

Oh, well. At least Nyree didn't have a roomie to ask inconvenient questions.

As she pulled out a duster and carefully stepped into an exhibition of polar explorer memorabilia, her mind slid to her mother's email. What the devil was Ari playing at involving her mother to get her to return to him? Toward the end, everything she'd done had upset him, so why would he want her back?

Control? More of her money? Nyree snorted in disgust. Both probably.

A reconciliation. She shook her head. Not happening. He'd never change, no matter his promises to the contrary.

Disgusted with the man all over again, Nyree shoved him from her mind and focused on the exhibition. A job here allowed her to get close to history, and she loved the novel way of learning. She studied a framed copy of Ernest Shackleton's bold, handwritten signature, the pair of woolen mittens, and the gabardine jacket that he or his expedition members had worn with a sense of awe.

At eleven, she stored her cleaning basket and prepared for the deluge of visitors. It was fun greeting the cruise ship passengers. Most were older since it was expensive to get to South Georgia and Antarctica. Soon men and women, most dressed in matching cruise ship-issued orange jackets, descended on her shop.

"Do you have a boyfriend?" a woman and one of her first customers asked. "My son is around your age."

"No boyfriend at the moment," Nyree said with a smile. "I'm too busy to look."

"You must get lonely here," another woman commented as she handed over a pile of postcards and a T-shirt to purchase.

"Not really." Nyree maintained her smile as she rang up the items. "We have a community of scientists, along with my coworkers. I do lots of walking and take photos, and this week, we're busy with ship visits."

The woman shuddered. "As much as this place is beautiful and interesting, I'd hate to live here for months on end without seeing friends, having a latte, or going to the local mall."

"I don't miss shopping, and it's an opportunity to save my wages."

The woman shook her head in clear doubt and gave way to the next customer. Nyree spent ten minutes running around after the elderly couple since they wanted to send postcards to their grandchildren and buy gifts for their children.

"We're on a retirement trip. I've always wanted to visit since my grandfather worked here at the whaling station," the thin and spare husband said.

His plump wife tsked. "We prefer seeing the whales swimming around in the ocean, but those were different times."

By the time the cruise ship left, the shelves bore empty spaces, and Nyree spent an hour refreshing the stock.

Carolyn appeared and came to a rapid halt in the doorway. "I was coming to help, but you've finished."

"Shouldn't I have restocked?" Nyree asked.

"Yes. No. I mean, you did the right thing. None of my previous helpers used their initiative. That's why I'm here. To issue orders and make certain we're ready for the next cruise ship. Great job. Is there anything else you need from the stockroom?"

"No, I made myself a list and have everything. I just need to fold these T-shirts to finish."

Carolyn beamed. "You've done well. I can't see a thing out of place. Thank you!"

"You don't have to thank me. I enjoy keeping busy, and besides, isn't this what you're paying me for?"

A laugh escaped Carolyn. "Some summer assistants haven't been as studious and do as little as they can."

"Oh. My mother taught my sister and me to pull our weight."

"You're a treasure. As soon as you finish here, why don't you go for a walk?"

"I'd like that. I didn't realize how much I'd enjoy taking wildlife photos and getting out for walks." Nyree checked the time. "I might do a longer hike. I'll pop in at your place at six to let you know I'm safely home."

"Perfect," Carolyn said. "Honestly, you've saved us so much work. It used to take me hours to restock, even with help. Enjoy your walk."

"I will." Nyree strode from the shop that doubled as the post office.

Today was perfect for a flight. She'd hike over the hill and soar over the island interior, far from prying eyes. For some reason, the discomfort in her belly was worse than usual, and a flight in her dragon form would go a long way to settling her taniwha moonlust.

Nyree pushed open the door to her accommodation and almost buckled at the knees. The intense wave of lust had her groaning, her nipples prickling to hard points. Hurriedly, she shut the door and breathed carefully through her mouth. The scent here differed from when she'd left. It smelled earthy and green, and it was the most enticing fragrance she'd inhaled for a long time.

She gulped, aghast at the dampness between her thighs, the sheer need throbbing through her sex. This was weird. She had to get out of here and shift before she did something dumb, like agree to join a scientist for a weekend of research.

Nyree forced her legs to move to her bedroom, where she changed into hiking clothes. She packed her jacket, her water bottle, and snack bars she'd brought from home. Flying always made her ravenous since her taniwha used lots of energy. She drew in more air. A mistake. Whatever the scent was, it was addictive, and she shuddered, her clothing cumbersome against her sensitized skin.

Hurriedly, she laced her hiking boots and stood. For an instant, she considered grabbing her vibrator and fixing the problem. No, a flight always worked best.

As soon as she entered the main lounge area, the scent jumped her again, and another groan squeezed past her clamped lips. She hesitated, buffeted by the strength of her need, and the intoxicating scent wafting from somewhere in her lounge. Part of her wanted to investigate while a saner part of her decided to flee.

Once she was outside, it took three deep inhalations to clear the sensual fog from her brain. Weird, since she'd never experienced the pull of the moon this badly. She set off with long strides, trotting up the rocky incline and passing the church. Ten minutes later, she was alone and more clear-headed. She kept walking, following the stream until she reached a sheltered spot she'd used in the past. Here, she removed her footwear and stripped. She tucked her clothes away in her daypack and stowed them.

Her shift was faster than expected and painful. Yet another groan spilled free before her transformation completed. She stood, slightly dazed before her wits returned. She'd never heard of another taniwha displaying the symptoms assailing her today. In theory, she should keep things together because of her regular flights. With a shrug, she studied the rolling lichen-covered hills and the mountain peaks beyond before she took to the air.

Nyree pushed herself hard, flying faster and farther than usual. The more exhausted she was after her flight, the better the results.

The crisp mountain air cleared her mind, and she enjoyed swooping over the mountain tops and exploring the hidden valleys. This high up, snow clung to the rocks. It was strange seeing no grass or trees, but the pristine environment and the privacy made up for the lack of greenery.

Once she returned to her bag, she dressed and took her time walking back to the township. She pulled out her camera and indulged herself in taking photos. Mainly she aimed her camera at the strutting penguins and the big-eyed seals, but she also took shots of the old rusted whaling equipment, the church, and the cemetery, which glistened in the late afternoon sun.

Just before six, she knocked on Carolyn's and Keith's door to let them know she'd safely returned.

"Stay for dinner," Carolyn said.

"Thanks, but I'm tired. I'm dreaming of a shower and an early night. I want to get up early and take photos of the sunrise."

"Better you than me," Keith said with a dry smile. "I stay in bed in the mornings for as long as possible."

"That's true," Carolyn agreed. "Wait for a few minutes, Nyree. I'll fix you a plate to take home with you."

"You don't have to do that," Nyree said.

"Let her fuss over you," Keith said. "Carolyn told me how well you fit in and how much work you're saving her. We appreciate your willingness to turn your hand to any job we throw your way."

"It's nothing," Nyree protested.

"Smell the pasta," Keith said. "My Carolyn does a great creamy pasta sauce. You can't tell us you're trying to diet because you're always away with that camera of yours and walking for hours."

Nyree shrugged. "I enjoy the peace here. The stark beauty and the penguins' and seals' antics amuse me. The albatross and the brown skua. Everything is new to me—magnificent and awe-inspiring."

Carolyn handed her a covered plate. "We appreciate your work ethic and the way you deal with our visitors. You don't flirt with the scientists or create friction. Believe me, you have no clue of the trouble one coquettish woman can create." Carolyn shooed her outside. "I'll see you in the morning."

Nyree waved and walked back to her accommodation. She passed a seal who tried to intimidate her with a direct charge. Nyree stood her ground, and the animal backed off, conceding. Keith had mentioned the seals became more aggressive during the breeding season.

She grinned. Little did these seals know. She was a bigger badass than them, and her taniwha would happily eat them for a snack. Her smile faded. She should've stood up for herself with Ari. No, Manu had told her she'd done the right thing protecting their secret. He and Hone had investigated Ari, and they'd agreed he'd be a problem if he'd discovered the existence of the taniwha race. Not that this dampened her regrets.

She should've handled Ari differently.

With a sigh, she pushed open her door. The earthy scent of lust had her gripping the door with her free hand.

What? How?

Nyree set the plate on the counter, and holding her breath, rushed to shove open the windows. One. Two. Three windows pushed wide to circulate fresh air.

She pivoted, ready to flee outside to rid her lungs of the seductive scent when a loud crash stopped her in her tracks. Her gaze darted toward the source of the sound, and her mouth dropped open. She blinked and refocused.

"What the hell?" she muttered.

CHAPTER 5

Miracle

A strange tingling passed through Tāwera, tightening his chest and confusing his mind. He'd suffered a similar upheaval on the day he'd become encased in stone. He had no clue what was happening now, and a healthy slice of fear trickled through him, mixing with the turmoil already bombarding his body.

Sharp, ominous, high-pitched screeches filled his ears, and they reverberated inside his head.

Snap! Crackle! Pop!

With each torturing shriek, a shard of pain burrowed into his body, his head. Tāwera struggled to avoid the phantom weapon, and each writhe increased the agony assailing him.

He was vaguely aware of the woman entering the room. He sensed rather than witnessed her run inside and shove open windows. The instant rush of breeze brought a delicate feminine fragrance to him. *Her scent.*

Without volition, he reached for her. Yet another booming crack, and Tāwera gasped. He'd swear a draft tickled his skin. His naked skin. He rotated his body, and the abrupt explosion had him freezing. Although pain still debilitated him, he forced his eyes open. His limbs and torso shifted with more fluidity and less constraint.

His heart beat so fast he worried it might leap from his chest.

Shock. Joy. Excitement. Fear.

Emotions buffeted him as he tried to understand how or why the stone encasing him was breaking off in large chunks.

A rush of energy pulsed, and this time Tāwera embraced pain as he flung around his arms and legs with far more vigor than he'd ever performed a *haka*. This was no war dance. This was a battle for his freedom.

Something had changed. Tāwera didn't know what, and he didn't care. If liberty tiptoed in his direction, he'd seize it and worry over the how and why later.

Tāwera pushed and shoved, and suddenly he was flowing freely like a patch of mist. Expanding and solidifying.

The woman—Nyree—croaked and backed up, her eyes wide.

Tāwera cleared his throat, his gaze now on a par with hers. Unlike most people of his long-ago acquaintance, she was almost as tall as him.

"Don't be frightened. I won't hurt you," Tāwera said.

When she stared blankly, he realized he'd spoken in Māori. He switched to the English taught to him by the missionaries.

"Nyree, my name is Tāwera. Please do not fear me. I promise I will never hurt you like the Ari-man."

Nyree gaped at the transparent man. Was he a genie? Did she get three wishes?

"What are you?" she muttered, too astonished to experience fear even though the man was tall and muscular and bore tattoos on his face. "A ghost?"

"No, I am Tāwera." He held up his arm and scowled. "A taniwha."

Nyree glanced over her shoulder to check outside her windows. Not a person in sight. "You can shift to a dragon?"

"Yes. At least I used to shift as much as possible without anyone learning of my true nature."

He'd spoken to her in Māori before switching to English. While she understood Māori, she wasn't fluent in her national language.

Before she reacted, he said, "You keep your identity a secret too."

"True. There are dozens of taniwha where I live, but most people ignore the old mythology and legends. They consider them interesting stories. In the world I come from, it's not safe to be different."

Tāwera frowned and slowly stretched. Although he was still see-through, she distinguished his form without difficulty. He brought to mind a warrior with his long black hair and full facial tattoos. He wore a *piupiu* tied around his waist—a garment made from individual strands of dried flax that swung and swished as he stretched. A cloak decorated with feathers hung around his shoulders, baring much of his chest. Her gaze drifted down to his bare feet.

She inhaled and caught the same scent that had upset her taniwha so severely when she'd first entered her home. It wasn't as concentrated this time, but it was every bit as seductive. She stepped closer without conscious thought. He was slightly taller than her. Taller than Ari. The flash of memory brought a wince, and she shoved Ari and the associated guilt and pain to the back of her mind. Instead, she focused on Tāwera. His skin color indicated Māori descent, but was he truly a taniwha?

"Are you frightened of me?" he asked, his voice husky and masculine, his golden brown gaze intense.

"No," she said without hesitation. It was the truth. While the situation was startling and unusual—magical—he didn't scare her.

His broad shoulders relaxed at her reply, and this time it was him who closed the gap between them. "Where am I?"

"You don't know?"

He shook his head.

"We're on South Georgia, which is near to Antarctica." His blank expression told Nyree she'd confused him. "I'll show you on a map. How did you get here?" Her stomach rumbled a hunger pang that was loud enough for Tāwera to hear.

"You are hungry. Eat food."

"All right," Nyree said, retreating. "Come with me. We'll sit at the table. Are you hungry? I'll share my pasta."

Tāwera followed, silent with his bare feet. She pulled out a chair at the scarred wooden table in her kitchen and indicated he should sit. As she'd suspected, Carolyn had sent her a huge helping, so she heated it and split the contents. Did ghosts eat? If that's what he was because, given his transparency, he wasn't exactly human either. A taniwha ghost. No one would give her the time of day with this revelation, even if she tried to explain.

"That smells good," he said, his gaze on the food. "What is it?"

"Pasta." Once she'd heated a portion, she gave it to him while she microwaved hers. When she went to join him, he was still staring at the food, and she realized she hadn't given him utensils. Nyree pulled two forks out of the drawer and handed him one. "We make pasta from flour, eggs, and water. The sauce is creamy, and Carolyn has added vegetables and sausage."

"Show me how to eat this," he said, his tone imperious.

"Like this," she said, demonstrating. "Asking questions or for examples is an excellent way to learn."

"My friends, my father, they would never ask," Tāwera replied, his tone blunt.

She waited until he'd taken his first mouthful. He chewed slowly, savoring before he swallowed. She hid a grin as his eyes widened, and he eagerly scooped up another bite. The food didn't reappear, so she figured *ghost* wasn't an apt description for him.

"Do you know how you arrived here in South Georgia?" she asked again.

"Yes." He ate more pasta before he spoke again. "I come from Aotearoa, land of the long white cloud."

"New Zealand," Nyree translated. "That is where I live too. Where in Aotearoa did you live?"

"*Kororāreka.*"

"North or South?" Nyree asked. She didn't recognize the place-name.

"North," Tāwera said.

"Can you tell me the neighboring towns?"

He rattled off several Māori names, but she recognized none of them.

"When did you leave your home to come here?"

"1780."

Nyree's fork stopped several inches from her mouth. She set the utensil back on her plate. "1780? That's hundreds of years ago." But it explained his use of the Māori language and his garments. His full facial tattoos. Few men tattooed their faces these days.

She trolled back through her hazy recollection of early New Zealand history. They had signed the treaty of Waitangi in 1840, and missionaries had arrived in the early 1800s. Perhaps earlier. She needed to research on the internet. The problem was access was patchy, given the variable weather and their remoteness. She started eating again, her thoughts busy. Maybe she'd email a list of questions to Emma. No, Manu was the better contact since he was a taniwha, and as head of their tribe, he'd want this information.

"How did you travel here?" Nyree asked.

"I came on a ship with a sailor who hunted for seals and sometimes whales," Tāwera replied without hesitation.

Okay. Sealers and whalers. They'd visited Russell in Northland to provision. They'd drunk and whored and earned Russell the name *hellhole of the Pacific*. She tried to recall the Māori name for Russell and failed. Another question to add to her list for Manu.

Nyree waited for Tāwera to tell her more, and when he didn't, she prompted him. "How did you get on the ship?"

Tāwera sighed and scowled at the remaining pasta on his plate. "It's a long story. I'd hate to spoil the first meal I've eaten since I can remember."

Nyree smiled. "Fair enough. Eat. We'll finish dinner, and you can tell me while we have coffee and a biscuit."

Tāwera frowned again and glanced askance at her. "I don't know this coffee."

"That's not important. You will learn quickly, although

explaining your presence to Keith and Carolyn might be tricky."

"I don't wish to create trouble."

"Eat," Nyree said, and her calmness surprised her. She was sitting down eating dinner with a ghost who appeared to be holding down food and enjoying it. *Peculiar*. She had to tell someone, or she'd burst. Manu, it was, then.

Once they'd eaten, Nyree placed their dirty dishes and utensils in the sink and boiled the jug to make instant coffee. Tāwera hovered nearby, watching her every action. Although it might've been creepy, the open curiosity she spotted in his golden brown eyes relaxed her. She opened a packet from her stash of chocolate biscuits and led the way to the lounge.

"This is coffee. It's a hot drink. The biscuits are sweet and go perfectly with the coffee."

"Thank you for sharing your meal with me," he said, his manner formal.

"You're welcome. You're going to repay me by appeasing my curiosity about how you traveled from New Zealand, I mean, Aotearoa to South Georgia and how you ended up inside the rock." She glanced at the fragments of rock still littering the worn brown carpet. "The gargoyle."

"Why did you call me George?"

Nyree grinned. "That's what you want to know," she teased. "Of all the questions you might ask."

"Yes." He didn't return her smile, but he didn't give off creepy vibes either.

"I called you George because I didn't know your name. Now I'll address you as Tāwera. I enjoyed talking to you, even though I might've sounded a little crazy. Giving you a name made you feel more like a friend."

He nodded, his gaze thoughtful. "I understand. Now it is my turn to talk. I lived with my tribe and was a successful warrior. My father was an important tribal leader with an influential position. My older brother, Rāwiri, was also of great consequence, especially given his age. He was a *tohunga*—an expert—of tattooing. He is...was gifted and did my tattoos. We had different mothers. Rāwiri's mother died in childbirth, and our father took my mother as his wife. Rāwiri was jealous of me."

Nyree sipped her coffee. "What happened?"

"I fell in love with the woman my brother coveted and wanted for his wife. I knew Rāwiri had approached Aroha's father, and her father approved the match, but Aroha and I... Rāwiri told me he understood and would stand aside to make his brother happy."

Nyree leaned forward, captured by the story. "What happened?"

"We planned a European marriage, with the ceremony the missionaries favored. A few weeks before the wedding, Rāwiri came to me and offered a gift between brothers. He told me he bore me no ill will and hoped we would always remain friends. Aroha and I were pleased because we didn't wish for family tension."

"Did he lie?"

"He did. His gift to me was a special tattoo. He showed me the design, and it was magnificent. He called it a wedding gift, but it was a curse. Too late, I realized this."

"How did the tattoo become a curse? Did he tattoo something else? Something offensive?"

"Worse, he wove a curse into the tattoo. When I went to Rāwiri's *whare* the night before our wedding for the final small part of the tattoo, the curse knit together and sucked me into the piece of stone he had sitting by his firepit. The agony that came with joining the various strands of the curse contorted my face and limbs. I fell unconscious, and when I came to my senses many hours later, Rāwiri had imprisoned me within the stone.

"Rāwiri spoke with me and joked. He knew I heard him and told me this was what happened when one attempted to go against a *tohunga*. Aroha visited to ask Rāwiri if he'd seen me. She came the next day—the day of our wedding—and she was crying because she thought I didn't wish the marriage any longer. Rāwiri comforted her in his arms. He held my Aroha and told her he was there for anything she needed. The entire time, he was watching me with this sly smile that was full of evil."

Nyree didn't understand why one brother would inflict that sort of torment on another. "Why wasn't he honest?"

"Rāwiri always held himself aloft from others. It was part of what made him an excellent *tohunga tā moko*, but once he'd cursed me, I remembered others speaking of bad luck after receiving a tattoo."

"Your brother did the same to them?"

"Perhaps. Rāwiri cursed me, so maybe he did the same to others."

Nyree stood. "Would you like more coffee?"

"Please," he said, extending his cup.

It occurred to her if he came from an earlier time, he wouldn't understand indoor plumbing, and she made a mental note to show him how everything worked. He'd eaten food, so she presumed his body would function in the same way as hers. He was still transparent, though. So many questions for Manu, including ones of cursed magical tattoos.

"Can I watch you make this drink?"

"You can do the work while I tell you what to do," she said. "It's interesting the way you can hold objects, although you still look like a ghost."

"A spirit?" he asked.

"Yes, I wonder if you're visible to others or just me." Nyree talked him through making coffee for both of them, and they returned to the lounge to drink it. "Tell me what happened next."

"I remember the pain and excruciating torment. The agony receded once he'd confined me to the stone. After our wedding day passed, Rāwiri took me or rather the stone into town, probably to dispose of me. Perhaps toss me in the sea. He met two sailors who wanted tattoos. Sometimes Rāwiri would lower himself to tattoo the visiting sailors to earn coins, so he usually took his tools with him whenever he walked into the township. While he was tattooing the sailor, his friend noticed me. He asked to buy my stone, and Rāwiri sold it to him as a souvenir of his visit to Aotearoa. A few days later, the sailor left on his ship, taking me with him. He sailed south, and then he moved to a sealing crew in a distant land. It's difficult for me to tell you where we went, but we followed the seals and the whales. Mostly, he worked for sealers, but he fished for whales at the last place."

"What happened to your sailor?"

"As he grew older, he became less nimble. A wave took him by surprise. He dropped me, and I never saw him again. I remained where I fell until you found me."

Nyree stared at Tāwera, curious about the history and events he'd witnessed from his prison. "Do you think your brother knew the curse could break?"

"No, he'd be furious to learn his magic failed," Tāwera said without hesitation. "He must never learn I am free."

Nyree bit her lip, tentative, but she had to give him the truth. "Tāwera, you last saw your brother in 1780. We're in the twenty-first century now." She hesitated. "Your brother and his family will be long dead. Aroha."

Tāwera blinked. "I hadn't considered this. You're right. Rāwiri and Aroha would no longer live. What am I going to do? All these years, I've wanted revenge, but if there is no one left, I have no purpose."

"Not true," Nyree said. "You live for the moment and enjoy what life you can have now."

"But how do I get home? I have no boat."

"We have other methods of transportation. If other people can't see you, you'll be able to walk onto a ship and travel to South America. From there, you transfer and fly to New Zealand."

His brows rose. "A flight?"

"Yes, men invented a machine that flies across the oceans. We have lots of ways to travel that are faster than walking."

"How will I learn these things? Everything is different. Your clothes, your food, and the way you live. Since you fished me from the sea, many things have astonished me. In my time, we walked or paddled our *wāka* around the coast. We hunted or grew our food. It did not come in those things you call packets."

Nyree scowled. "You'll also need money. I'd give you some, but Ari stole most of what I'd saved."

"What is money?"

"The same as the coins you mentioned that the sailors gave your brother. When we want something—maybe food or clothing or to travel on a ship or airplane, we must pay money for the goods."

"It is like trading our surplus goods for something else from another tribe?"

"Yes, that's correct," Nyree said. "I understand how disorientating my world must seem to you, but you'll find some things are the same. We use machines and computers to do tasks that once might have taken days or months to complete, which means we have more leisure time to do things we enjoy. I go walking or take photos." Nyree patted Tāwera's forearm and lifted her fingers from his skin as quickly as she'd placed them there.

Tāwera sucked in an audible breath while Nyree fought the need to wrap her arms around him to experience the sensation again. She'd tingled, and it had been like a sharp slap—the foreign rush in her blood and the physical surge of desire. When she risked a glance at him, he seemed equally shocked. She backed up and forced herself to calm.

Tonight, she'd write an email to Manu and pray he'd get back to her with answers because she had no idea of what to do with this handsome taniwha ghost.

CHAPTER 6

Modern Exploration

The next morning.

"What will I do while you do this work thing?" Tāwera asked while Nyree was staring at something she'd called a tablet.

"I'm uncertain if other people see you. You seemed more solid last night, but this morning you've faded again. I have no idea what this means because you don't have problems picking up items or eating."

Tāwera held up his almost transparent arm and said what they were both pondering. "Will I fade away until no one can see me? Not even you?"

Nyree shrugged and placed her tablet on a shelf. "I'd hoped my friend would've emailed by now. A few messages have come through, so the connection is working. Why don't you come with me? I can show you around, and you can explore on your own while I'm working."

"I would enjoy that." He hadn't wanted to stay cooped up inside, not after years of nothingness and defined boundaries. Now was the perfect time to indulge his senses in a way he hadn't for hundreds of years.

"You should try to shift to your taniwha and explore the island, but don't go too crazy. Okay?"

Eagerness pulsed in him. Excitement at the freedom after confinement inside his stone prison. "I could do that? Shift?"

"Yes, except you won't be able to leave the island until we figure out how to get you home, but you can explore and watch the other people who visit. You have time to decide on the next step. The summer season ends in March, which is when we all leave. If you're invisible, a cruise ship or a supply vessel might be the best way for you to travel home."

Tāwera frowned, not understanding most of Nyree's conversation. "I hope I learn fast."

"You will," she said with a smile. "Do you want breakfast?"

"My stomach is empty."

"Okay then. This is breakfast cereal, and I usually have toast as well."

They worked together to make breakfast, with Nyree showing him how to work the toasting machine and serve the cereal. He watched closely and copied her actions, smelling the white rice bubbles. A scent didn't jump out at him, but the toast excited him more when Nyree spread something called crunchy peanut butter on the top.

He'd dreamed about what he might do once he broke the curse, but eating toast and cereal or spending time with a beautiful woman had never entered his mind. It had never occurred to him he might miss hundreds of years, and everyone he'd known would have long ago died. Aroha... A twinge of pain worked through him at her loss. He'd wondered about her often and prayed she'd had a happy life. Thinking of her now and knowing she was long dead, his feelings toward her were more bittersweet, a mourning for the young girl he'd held in his arms. The long-ago memories. Thoughts of his brother, however, made him burn with anger. Tāwera burned to understand how his brother had structured this curse. Had he known a stranger might break it?

"Why are you scowling like a warrior about to go into battle?"

"Even now, I'm shocked by my brother's actions. I considered us friends. We trod different paths, and our father ignored us both. Rāwiri had no reason to resent me."

"Your fiancée," she reminded him.

"I wonder what happened to her. I hope she was happy."

"That was one of the questions I asked Manu."

A growl rattled deep in his throat, and he took half a step toward Nyree before his mind understood what he was doing. Nyree stilled, her expression watchful.

Slowly, he raised his hands, palms extended outward in a position of surrender. "I promise never to hit or knowingly hurt you."

"Why did you snarl?" She straightened and shot him a glower. "That's not civilized. You're a taniwha. If you strike me, I will retaliate in kind."

She looked cute. Aroha had been sweet and loving, but she hadn't possessed Nyree's inner core of strength. Her fire.

Nyree advanced on him and poked his chest with her forefinger. A dart of pain accompanied by more awareness had him gasping.

"You feel solid enough," she said, her tone rueful as she wriggled her finger with care.

A tremor passed through him as he inhaled her clean scent, and he fought the urge to embrace her and press their mouths together in the way of the Europeans. He and Aroha had tried this many times. Aroha hadn't enjoyed the contact of lips and the tangle of tongues as much as he. His gaze drifted to Nyree's lush mouth, and he leaned closer, only to jerk upright when she poked him in the chest again.

He fingered the sore spot. "That hurts."

"It's meant to divert your attention to answering my question."

"What question?" His gaze had developed a will of its own.

In his defense, her lips looked soft, which made him curious and yearn to explore.

"Why did you growl at me?"

Tāwera gave her truth. "I don't enjoy you mentioning other men."

"What?" She sounded incredulous.

Tāwera swallowed, unable to explain the burst of his emotions. "You rescued me, gave me a roof and food."

"I expect nothing in return. Now hurry and finish eating. I don't want to be late for work."

Confusion dulled his reaction time, and he continued to stare at her.

"Tāwera, did you hear me?"

"What? Yes." This reaction was an unusual one for him—the hesitation. He was—had been—a leader. Someone who made decisions. He'd never hesitated but moved onward, always trusting his gut instinct. Right now, he teetered as if he stood in a swamp, and any of his next steps might send him waist-deep into the mud.

Aware of Nyree's impatience, he drank his coffee and ate the last mouthful of toast covered with something black called vegemite. It was salty and bore an interesting flavor, although he'd liked the peanut butter better. He stood. "Should I do the dishes?"

Nyree laughed. "We'll do them later."

"Why are you laughing? Should I not offer? Is doing dishes women's work?"

"These days, men and women share tasks." As she spoke, Nyree placed containers away in cupboards and the refrigerator.

His mind buzzed with information and the differences between his world then with now.

Nyree glanced at the timepiece she wore on her wrist and moved even faster. "Let's go."

Tāwera dutifully followed her outdoors and took pleasure in the chilly wind against his chest.

Nyree walked beside him and pointed out the landmarks. Tāwera craned his neck to study the enormous pieces of machinery.

"White men like the sailor who brought you here fished for whales in this bay. They captured thousands and almost decimated the population. These days it is illegal to capture whales, and slowly, the population has increased. Once we go flying together, I'll show you the whales. Some days they play in the water and show off. Have you seen penguins before?"

"Once. Mostly, I heard them," Tāwera said. "I am also familiar with seals."

"All right. This is the museum. Can you read English?"

"The missionaries taught me."

"Excellent. You'll be able to read the descriptions in the exhibits. They explain each display. You might like to explore that while I'm busy in the gift shop. Carolyn mentioned a cruise ship is arriving in around an hour. You should find plenty to keep you amused."

"Nyree." A woman appeared from another room. She glanced

left and right. "Who were you talking to?"

"Myself," Nyree said without hesitation. "I get better answers that way, Carolyn."

Carolyn blinked as Tāwera moved to stand beside Nyree. For an instant, he wondered if the woman saw him, but she laughed and stared right through him.

Tāwera puffed out a harsh breath, his chest growing tight. It had been too much to hope others might see him. He was lucky he had Nyree to speak with and to show him the modern ways.

"Did you have something specific you wanted me to do today? I was going to double-check the stock levels in the store, then do a walk-through of the museum to make certain everything is ready for our next visitors."

Carolyn laughed. "I don't know why I bother checking on you. You do everything I need to do without being asked." She turned to return before pausing. "The other temp worker scheduled to arrive in two weeks rang this morning. She can't come since her mother has cancer. Suzie needs to remain at home to look after her mother."

"Oh, I'm very sorry," Nyree said.

"They're going to find a replacement, but I told Brett, the organizer, we were doing fine at present."

While Nyree chatted with the woman, Tāwera wandered around the building's interior and studied everything with interest.

Pictures covered the walls, and everything appeared tidy and smelled inoffensive. Machines sat on desks and in corners, and Tāwera marveled at the things these people used to make their lives easier.

"I'll check in with you later, once the passengers come ashore, in case you need help."

"I'll be fine," Nyree said. "It's easy and nothing compared to working in a busy pub."

"If you're sure," Carolyn said. "Would you like to take control of a tour this afternoon?"

"I'd love to," Nyree said.

"Right. I'll let you know the time."

Tāwera waited until the woman left before speaking to Nyree. "She didn't see me."

"No, but I wonder if she can hear you. The shop is this way, near to the museum. We sell books, T-shirts, postcards, stamps, and a few other things. The visitors like to send cards and letters home to their families."

To Tāwera, this was a mystery, but he figured he'd learn. "Can I help you?"

"Sure, you can carry the heavier boxes for me, so I don't need to make lots of trips." She grinned at him, an impish grin that shouted mischief.

She hadn't looked this way when she'd received the message about the Ari-man. His nostrils flared, and his muscles tensed.

"What's wrong? I've seen you carry the plates and cutlery. Are you worried this won't work? No matter what, we'll help you get home. No one should have to suffer a curse like this and especially one because of plain jealousy."

Her concern and reassurance wiped away his stormy thoughts. "Sorry. Sometimes I slip and feel miserable and angry about my situation. My apologies." There was no way he'd confess he was furious on her behalf. He'd known warriors who spoke with their fists, especially after drinking the white man's stinking water.

"That's understandable." She unlocked a door and led the way into a long, low building with a flat roof. "This is our wee shop. Mostly, it's the T-shirts and postcards I need to restock." She reached down and lifted a brown box before walking toward Tāwera. "See the empty gaps in this rack?"

The words she used were unfamiliar, but Tāwera soon understood what she wanted of him after she'd demonstrated the task.

"Oh. One thing." She flashed another impish grin. "You'd better watch for people walking past. It will shock them to see postcards floating through the air."

"I can do that." Tāwera spent an enjoyable ten minutes studying the bright pictures and filling the gaps. "I'm finished."

"Perfect timing," Nyree said, glancing out their windows. "It looks as if the first load of passengers has arrived."

"What should I do?"

"Wander around and explore. Listen to the passengers. Try talking to one of them to work out if they can hear you." She wrinkled her nose. "Don't scare anyone too much."

Tāwera nodded, suddenly eager to test the boundaries of this strange world.

Nyree flapped her hands at him. "Go. I'll be here if you need me for anything. If you have questions, it's best to save them for later when we're alone."

"My thanks, Nyree."

"You're welcome. Go."

The door opened behind him, and two women wearing bright yellow jackets wandered inside. They wore hats and scarves wound around their necks.

"Postcards!" one cried. "Can we mail them here?"

Nyree smiled at them. "We operate as a post office and a store."

Tāwera slipped through the open door and studied the new arrivals who wandered past him.

Curious about the men of this time, he attached himself to a group of males and followed them as they explored the old whaling equipment. Several of them stopped to point small machines in different directions, and he made a note to ask Nyree what they were doing. Most of the visitors had these machines.

"Louise is gorgeous," one said. "Does she have a boyfriend?"

"Yeah, she has a man at home," a second man said.

"Might try my luck, anyway. Louise lives in the same suburb as me."

Tāwera grinned, understanding that the dance between male and female was the same as when he had been a young warrior despite the different times and the unusual machines.

He wandered on to eavesdrop on another group walking to the church. The wind ruffled and tugged at his topknot, and the chill pebbled his skin, yet he continued with his explorations, despite the low temperatures. Each flex of his muscles proved he was alive, and it was a magical sensation with the breeze tickling his flesh and the scent of rain riding the air.

"It's going to rain," he said.

"Really?" a short woman asked. Her almost square shape intrigued him. "The clouds aren't dark, and the captain never mentioned rain. I'm certain he would've told us if poor weather was on the horizon."

"I can smell the rain," Tāwera said and moved on before the woman realized he was invisible. He found if he concentrated, he comprehended most people. Some even spoke like the visitors to his town—the men from the faraway land of France.

Tāwera continued walking and followed a line of yellow-clad people up a hill. Here, the wind blew wilder and more fiercely, reminding him of the freedom of flying. Without hesitation, he strode from the group to seek a sheltered spot to leave his clothes. He stripped off his cloak, the sandals Nyree had found him, *piupiu*, and undergarments and stuffed them in a crevice. To make sure his possessions didn't blow away, he placed a rock over the top. Naked, he stood poised on the hillside while he centered his mind and called up his taniwha.

His muscles and bones reshaped, starting his change, but it was sluggish. For an instant, worry coalesced in his heart. Would he shift, or was this form cursed too?

Focus.

Memories of his mother stilled his panic. She'd shown him how to transform and explained how the moon's pull affected their species. When they shifted, their taniwha remained stable, but if they couldn't change because of a compromising position, once they became adults, they needed sexual release during the time of the full moon.

At least that was one problem that hadn't surfaced during his confinement.

His thoughts slipped to Nyree, then meandered on to the demands of the taniwha. How did she remain level during the full moon? Here, she could shift, but what happened to taniwha in the larger towns and the places Nyree called cities? Another question for his list.

His wings burst from his shoulders, and the jolt of agony almost buckled his knees. He sank to the rocky ground, his breathing hoarse and labored. The pain was so intense, Tāwera struggled to hold the image of his dragon in his mind. Just when he thought he might blackout, his shift burst through him.

Exhausted but elated, he pushed to his knees, his taniwha senses keener than he recalled. The urge to fly batted at him, along with a foreign blast of fury.

His dragon.

Tāwera sucked a breath into his big lungs, his scaled chest rising and falling, then muscle memory had him taking to the air. He turned into the breeze, allowing the wind to aid his flight. This first time his flight would need to be short. Tāwera glanced down at the sea glistening beneath him. Not the wisest course. He should've thought harder and remained on land. If he went into the sea, he wouldn't have the energy to swim. Too late now.

He flapped his wings and realized that already he had traveled a distance out to sea. Fighting the wind, he turned in an arc. The ship bobbed beneath him, and his mind darted to a viable solution. Land on the ship to rest and recover. He'd steal aboard a small boat from the ship and ride to shore with the passengers. If that didn't work, he'd fly after a brief rest. His belly rumbled. Yes, after a rest, perhaps he'd pilfer food. That would help with his low energy.

Pleased to have a plan, Tāwera directed his body toward the ship.

His landing wasn't pretty since his wings gave out. Only sheer determination kept him gliding as far as the open deck. He thumped down, and a passenger who was standing at the ship railing let out a surprised squeal. She half fell against the siding. The ship rolled before bobbing and righting itself, and other people screeched when an enormous wave created by his sudden landing almost upended their tiny boat. Tāwera's muscles quivered, but he forced himself to grab the female and shunt her toward the safety of a doorway that led inside the ship.

She screamed again, right in his ear, as he yanked at the door with his foreleg.

Luckily, the woman didn't struggle too much as he shoved her through the gap. As he slumped against the doorway, blocking the exit, he noted the scurry of men and women inside the cabin. The raised, excited voices.

A soft groan squeezed up his throat, and every part of his dragon body ached. Tāwera closed his eyes, unable to do more than rest. He shuddered to imagine what might have happened had he not grabbed the woman in time. He hadn't meant to place her in danger.

The shunt in the middle of his back had him jerking from the state of partial slumber. A second jolt woke him right up, and he roared, flames tearing from his open maw.

CHAPTER 7

A Dragon Calamity

Nyree stepped outside during a quiet moment, enjoying the whiff of sea air and the faint underlying pong of penguin droppings. With one eye on the open shop door, she scanned her surroundings, searching for Tāwera.

A burst of screams and whoops had her gaze snapping toward the beach.

A wave, larger than usual, crashed to shore, causing pandemonium amongst the seals and wooly brown king penguin chicks who'd congregated on the beach. Squawks and the *peep-peep* of panicked chicks filled the air while the seals grunted and barked in alarm when the wave washed them off their sunning rocks.

Excited voices filled the air, and Nyree locked the door and bolted toward the beach.

She met Keith and Carolyn and two of the scientists.

"What's happening? Is everyone all right?" Nyree gasped out.

"It was a rogue wave," Doug, a scientist, said. His dark hair stuck up as if he'd forgotten to comb it this morning.

"Should we be evacuating the beach?" Carolyn asked. "What if it's a tsunami?"

"I checked," Roger, the other portly scientist, said. "No earthquake reports anywhere."

Each of them eyed the beach and the sea. The cruise ship crew also scanned for more waves, having suspended their operations as a precaution.

Nyree didn't see Tāwera, which worried her a little.

No, he was an intelligent adult, despite his lack of modern life knowledge.

A roar interrupted her thoughts.

"What is that?" Carolyn asked. "Is it another wave?"

"The sea is flat," Doug replied, his hand disordering his hair as he tugged at his fringe.

"Look," Keith said, shock making his voice shake.

Nyree stared at the cruise ship anchored offshore. Flames shot from the rear deck, and another roar echoed through the bay. She swallowed.

So that was where Tāwera had gone.

"Where are the flames coming from?" a blonde in charge of an inflatable asked. She plucked a radio off her belt and called the ship.

"Are they all right?" Keith asked her.

"No injuries. The captain says something is blocking the rear deck exit, but he can't work out why the door refuses to open. The ship isn't on fire." She shook her head as she relayed her conversation to a colleague. "The captain says the fire doesn't seem dangerous. It's not burning anything. It's a mystery."

Nyree might have an inkling as to the cause. At least Tāwera wasn't damaging the ship, but the roar had been one of pain. She hesitated, wavering over what to do.

The blonde woman's radio crackled to life. "We have the flames under control, and there's no damage. The crew has investigated outside and doesn't know what caused the noise or the fire. Captain reports we can resume operations."

Nyree slumped for an instant before straightening. "I'd better reopen the shop. Let me know if there are any more problems or if I need to shut."

Carolyn patted her arm. "Will do."

Nyree strode toward the shop, searching the vicinity as she returned to work. "Tāwera, what are you doing?" she muttered. "You'd better not be causing trouble."

Tāwera inhaled and pushed the breath back out, repeating this several times to slow the race of his thudding heart. He had to move out of the way before the humans became more upset. Another growl struggled for freedom, but he swallowed it down and crawled away from the doorway. Each move produced new darts of pain to poke at his muscles.

He'd never suffered such as this with his energy sapped and every muscle on fire.

The instant he moved, humans burst outside. They wore uniforms and concerned expressions. Tāwera wanted to growl again while his throat tickled with the beginnings of flames. He dragged in a deep breath and scrambled away from two men examining the railings and the floor.

He tried to shift to his human form, but his bobbling and fractured mind mucked up his concentration. Heat built in his throat until his flames burned for release. He used his energy to scramble to his feet and directed the fire into the air.

The two men shouted, their bodies jolting in surprise. They rushed toward him, and one stood on his tail. Distress rocketed through him, and a roar of agony escaped. Flames chased his cry up his throat. The human fell off-balance and toppled on his butt. He released a shout of his own while the other man scrambled backward. He bumped into Tāwera and let out a muffled *oomph*.

"What the hell was that?" the first man asked.

The second man rubbed his wide eyes. "No idea. I'd swear I

walked into a wall."

"I tripped on something." He scowled at the deck while Tāwera tried to distance himself and drag his abused body farther away. The tickling in his throat resumed, and he gave an involuntary hiccup. A spark sizzled in the air before vanishing.

"Did you see that?"

The two men exchanged a glance, and the other one nodded.

"What is it?" the first man whispered.

"I don't know, but I hope it doesn't set our ship on fire." He rubbed at his eyes and blinked. "It's kinda hard to take action when we can't see what to fix."

"Yeah."

Tāwera needed to find a safe place to rest and let his body heal. He forced his torso upward and scanned the deck for a place safe from clumsy humans. If he stopped spurting fire, he could get inside and search out a peaceful spot in which to recover.

His taniwha wasn't right.

Whether it was the curse or the lack of flying, he didn't know, but staying here with vulnerable humans might mean injuries. None of this was their fault.

A door opened behind him, and Tāwera propelled his body across the deck and through the gap before he second thought the idea. He bowled over the woman who tried to come through, and the two male humans raced over to help her to her feet.

Sorry. Regret filled Tāwera at her pained shout. He hiccupped twice, his eyes widening at the sparks that shot toward the curtains. Hands. *Hands.* He needed hands.

Panic filled him as he struggled to visualize his human form. Holes burned in the fabric, and a glow formed around the edges. He smelled smoke, and his panic increased. *Don't set the boat on fire.* His sailor had feared fire, carrying the scars of a sea mishap when the ship he'd traveled on had burned and sunk.

Concentrate.

Nyree counted on him. No, confusion mired his mind. He relied on Nyree. Yes, that was what he meant.

Some of his panic faded, the tension leaching from his muscles. He wanted to get to know Nyree better because she was an intriguing woman. Nyree's form slid into his mind readily enough, not even the shouts and cries from the humans breaking the mental vision of her loveliness.

A human woman rushed toward him and threw her drink at the curtain.

Tāwera didn't know what was in the drink, but it worsened the situation. The smoldering fabric burst into flames. He gasped. His elbows pressed into his sides while he blinked rapidly.

Shift. Shift. *Shift.*

He tried to picture his two-legged form to start his transformation, but that didn't work. He squeezed his eyes shut and attempted to block out the fire, the humans, the acrid smoke. *Focus!* If he couldn't hold his form in his mind, what if he imagined

Nyree with him standing beside her?

His muscles tightened as his tension grew. Another human stood on his tail, and he choked back his tortured cry. Instead, he curled in a tight ball and focused on Nyree. Once he had her fixed in his mind, he concentrated on adding himself to the picture. Lightheaded elation filled him as this plan worked. He attached to the mental vision and willed his taniwha body to change. As with his shift from human to dragon, the transformation was labored.

But it worked.

His legs refused to hold his weight, and he toppled on his arse, but he didn't care. He'd shifted to taniwha and back to his human form.

Success.

"Did you hear that?" a woman whispered.

Tāwera lifted his head, more alert now. Every human in the large room—he was uncertain of the cabin's purpose—stared in his direction, but they didn't see him. He pushed to his feet and stayed upright, despite his trembling knees. At least the pain had subsided once he'd morphed back to two legs. It didn't hurt to breathe now. Each even inhalation filled his nostrils with sea air and helped his ruffle thoughts to settle.

Nyree had suggested he experiment. Right now, he wanted to learn if his shift to dragon and back had changed anything else apart from his pain levels. Could these people see him? He scanned the room's occupants and approached the smaller group who stood closer to an open doorway. He required an escape route in case the humans panicked. Tāwera sidled nearer, curious since they chattered like a morning chorus of birds. They spoke the French language, but he had difficulty understanding every word. They used their hands in tiny gestures, their faces expressive as they burst into laughter.

Tāwera cleared his throat and yanked a few French words from his rusty mind. "*Bonjour.*"

The laughter cut off, leaving the room strangely silent.

Tāwera spoke again. "Good morning. How are you today?"

"Was that you, Georges?" a woman asked in a hushed voice. Her eyes were so wide, Tāwera wondered if they might pop out and roll across the smooth wooden floor.

"Not I," a gangly man said and tugged his right ear.

"Can you hear me?" Tāwera asked, impatient with their astonishment. Why didn't they answer?

"Y-yes," one young woman replied. Her face had turned so pale dozens of golden spots on her nose and cheeks became stark and visible.

"What is your name?" Tāwera asked, directing his question to the lady with the face dots.

"J-Julia?" Her name emerged as a question rather than a statement. "Are you playing a joke on us?"

This question came out in a rush, and Tāwera spotted a tic in her jaw. Her hands clenched at her sides.

"No, my name is Tāwera. Thank you for speaking with me." Satisfied that others understood him, he turned away.

Every instinct told him he needed to rest before attempting to reach the shore, so he set out to explore the ship. Nothing about this vessel resembled the others he'd traveled on with the sailor.

Tāwera wandered through another doorway. The wooden floor changed from hard to soft—the carpet, the curtains, the ornaments and flowers, the chandeliers—were far more luxurious than the basic ship he'd first traveled on with his sailor. He peeked through open doorways and followed a young man around as he tidied and cleaned what looked like a combination bedroom and lounge. He needed to ask Nyree what they called this style of room.

When the man left, Tāwera hurriedly followed. He yanked at the door, relieved when it opened to his touch. When he stepped outside, he spotted the young man again, standing in the middle of the corridor. His expression held shock and astonishment, along with a healthy dose of fear.

"I'm sorry for frightening you," Tāwera said and patted the man's shoulder. A hint of lemon and something stronger, more astringent, wafted from the man as Tāwera walked past more doors. It looked as if this section of the ship contained more rooms in the same style as the one he'd just explored.

A thump had Tāwera pivoting in his tracks. The young man sprawled on the floor, and Tāwera rushed to his side, concerned he'd suffered an injury. His breath was warm against Tāwera's palm. Perhaps Tāwera should get someone to help the man, and then he'd venture onward to explore more of the intriguing ship.

Tāwera jogged back in the direction he'd come from and found a group of people talking to a lady behind a counter. At least that is what Nyree had called the arrangement. "Excuse me," he said. "A man is lying on the floor down that passage. He does not seem well."

The group fell silent. Not a one moved.

"The man is sick," Tāwera barked, and he watched a man spring into action. Reassured something was happening, Tāwera went on his way. He smelled food, and his stomach let out a happy rumble of encouragement. From memory, hunger always struck him after a shift. He'd made it a point to eat as soon as possible to rebuild his strength.

As Tāwera followed the food scents, he was aware of another urgent prickling. The tug of the moon. Did this mean his taniwha would force a shift in a few nights? No fair maidens were vying for his attention, so satiating his dragon in this manner was not possible. Not unless Nyree wished...

No!

Tāwera refused to make her do anything against her will.

His brow wrinkled as he tugged at the thoughts. If he wasn't mistaken, a storm rode on the air. He should discuss this with Nyree while they were both rational and not driven by moonlust.

Yes. Nyree had informed him men and women had frank

discussions, or at least she'd mentioned most happy people had open communication, so he would approach this subject with the honesty she'd told him was healthy.

Tāwera continued to climb the stairs in search of the delectable scents. They were unlike anything he'd smelled before, but it was definitely food. Nyree had described her life and the ways of humans, but seeing the truth for himself was still mind-opening.

He spotted a man with a strange, tall white hat. He'd dressed in clothes of the same color and carried a platter piled with food. Tāwera hustled to catch up because his curiosity was a huge thing. He followed the man through another doorway, and the scents that struck him had him halting in astonishment. He'd never seen so much food in one place. Not even when the tribe had a *hāngī* was there such a display. The thought had him adding another question to his list. He needed to ask if their people still cooked their food in a *hāngī,* steaming it in the ground.

What he wouldn't give to taste the smoky goodness of the meat and *kūmara* again.

The man settled his plate amongst the others and strode toward Tāwera. Tāwera hurriedly stood aside to avoid a collision. Once the man vanished, Tāwera wandered down the line of food. Beautifully arranged, it was a feast for his eyes. His belly released another rumble, and Tāwera chose a piece of food. He did not know what it was, and at this stage, he didn't care, given his powerful hunger.

A chunk of white meat. A yellow vegetable. A red vegetable.

Each bite tasted interesting and satisfying. Some foods crunched while others melted on Tāwera's tongue.

He spotted a pile of plates and took one. Every offering enticed him, and he was eager to sample everything. Soon, he'd heaped his platter, and he retreated to find a place to sit. Ah! A knife and fork. He and Nyree had used them while dining the previous evening. It was etiquette.

Tāwera sat and surveyed his meal with satisfaction, then he began eating. He ate slowly, despite the ominous grumblings of his belly. This was an experience he did not wish to hurry, and he savored every mouthful. He wished Nyree was here to share this meal. Perhaps he'd take some of the delicious fare with him. They had plenty, and Tāwera was positive the people here wouldn't miss a plate of food.

Something crashed to the floor behind him, and Tāwera turned, his fork suspended in the air. He discovered two men staring at him, trays of food splattered on the floor at their feet.

"I am sorry to disturb you," Tāwera said. "I was hungry, and there is plenty of food. Enough to feed everyone."

One man—a short, wiry man, dressed in white—released a hair-raising scream and fled. The other seemed made of sterner stuff, and he warily approached while Tāwera continued eating. He wore an eyepiece below his bushy black brows and had a round face.

"Ah, how long have you been here?" the man asked finally.

"I am visiting," Tāwera said. "I will leave once I have regained my strength."

The man crossed himself in the same way the churchmen had when they'd witnessed something they disapproved of, and it made Tāwera laugh.

"Are you a ghost?" the man asked.

"No." Tāwera straightened, his chin lifting. "I am a taniwha." *Oh! He shouldn't have mentioned that. Perhaps the man would forget.*

The man scowled and glanced over his shoulder at four other men, also dressed from head to foot in white. They drew closer, but each looked terrified.

"You will leave once you've eaten?"

"Yes, I must get back to the land." Tāwera had wanted to mention Nyree, but he hated to get her into trouble. It was best if these humans did not learn of their connection.

"All right," the man said, pushing at the center of his eyepiece. "Would you like dessert and cheese and biscuits to finish? A cup of coffee before you leave or some dessert wine?"

Tāwera considered his almost empty plate. "Yes, please." Another thought occurred. "Could you prepare food for me to take with me?"

The man tugged at his own hands and bit his lip. "Y-you won't come back and frighten our passengers?"

103

"No, I will not return. I will require rest," Tāwera said.

"D-do you promise this?"

"Yes," Tāwera said. "What is your name?"

"Ernesto." The man wrung his hands but did not retreat.

"Thank you, Ernesto. You are a kind man." Tāwera finished his last mouthful and set his eating utensils across the center of his plate as Nyree had shown him. "I am ready for more food now."

"I-I will bring you dessert. Frank, a coffee for the gentleman, please. Do you take milk?"

Tāwera considered this and remembered he had this morning. He would take his coffee this way again. "Yes, please."

"Frank, a coffee with milk for the gentleman. Tony, prepare a plate of cheese and biscuits while I dish up dessert."

Two men hustled to follow Ernesto's orders while the other two remaining whispered together with increasing agitation.

Tāwera cocked his head, their voices audible because of his excellent taniwha senses.

"I can see him. He's naked!" one said.

"We'll have to fumigate the chair," the other muttered.

"Here is your dessert. I hope you enjoy the selection I've chosen for you." Ernesto set the plate in front of Tāwera and stepped back with a scowl. "You are becoming visible. Your form is faint, but I am certain you weren't discernable earlier."

Tāwera lifted his arm and frowned. Ernesto was right. "Maybe it is your excellent food, but whatever the reason, this is an interesting turn of events."

"Perhaps you should complete your meal and leave. We do not wish to upset the passengers."

"May I take my cheese and biscuits with me? Perhaps enough for two persons?" Tāwera asked.

Ernesto gulped, his brows almost a solid line across his forehead, so deep was his frown. "There are two of you?"

"Yes," Tāwera said and dug into his dessert. He groaned with pleasure at the first mouthful. This was delicious. He continued eating while the men in white fluttered around him, halting often to whisper and stare at each other. One brought out a tiny machine and directed it at Tāwera.

"Look at the tattoos on his face," a man with a rounded stomach muttered.

"I've never seen anything like this," another breathed. He pulled out a small object and aimed it in Tāwera's direction. The man's hands trembled, and he cursed to himself, using the Lord's name in vain. The missionaries would not have approved.

"I have packed cheese and biscuits for you." Ernesto fluttered his hands. "H-how did you get here? I mean, how will you leave with no one seeing you?"

Tāwera savored the last mouthful of a cake. He didn't know what it was, but it was brown and tasted like nothing he'd ever eaten before. "I will fly," he said absently.

"F-fly?" Ernesto stuttered.

Tāwera straightened. He should not have said that either. *Concentrate!* A glance at his arm told him he must attempt to get to shore now before he became even more noticeable.

"Fly?" Ernesto repeated.

"Yes." Tāwera stood. "Thank you for the food. It was delicious. I must leave now."

"C-can you hold this while er...flying, or should I place it inside a bag?"

Tāwera considered the box. "A bag with handles would be most helpful. Thank you, Ernesto."

Ernesto snapped his fingers. "A bag. There is a cloth one hanging behind the kitchen door. Please bring it immediately." He turned his attention back to Tāwera. "Do you require a quiet place from which to leave?"

"Yes." Tāwera beamed at Ernesto, liking this man's commonsense nature. "As long as I have an open area, I should manage to take off." He *would* take off. He must return to Nyree.

"We will go to the bridge," Ernesto told him. "There is an area in front with the space you require."

A man returned with a bright blue bag and handed it to Ernesto. Ernesto packed the box inside and gave it to Tāwera.

"Thank you," Tāwera said.

"If you would come this way." Ernesto set off at a brisk pace, and Tāwera broke into a trot to catch up. The other men scuttled out of their way.

"He has tattoos on his buttocks, too," one man cried.

Didn't everyone? Yet another question to ask Nyree. He had seen no one else with *moko* like him. Not even Nyree had the traditional chin *moko* that most adult Māori women of his acquaintance sported. He must ask Nyree about this.

"Ernesto?" a male voice asked.

"I have an unauthorized guest who assures me he can fly to the land. I thought it best to bring him to the front deck where fewer people would spot him," Ernesto said, speaking so fast his words almost tripped over each other.

"Unauthorized? How did he get onto the ship? Wait, fly?" the unseen man spluttered.

"Yes, please stand back, and you will understand what I mean." Ernesto paused before glancing over his shoulder and gesturing for Tāwera to follow him.

"Jesus Christ," a voice said.

"No, I am Tāwera. I am pleased to meet you."

A thump greeted his words, the man sliding to the floor in a heap.

"Is he all right?" Tāwera asked.

"I will see to him," Ernesto promised. "It is best for you to leave now. The passengers must be aboard by three. Then we leave to visit our next stop."

Tāwera nodded since Nyree had explained this to him.

They walked outside.

"I will need you to hold the bag while I shift," Tāwera instructed. "Please stand right where I am now. Once I take to the air, I will pluck the bag from your hand. Thank you once again for the meal. I enjoyed it immensely."

Ernesto nodded. "You are welcome." He accepted the bag from Tāwera.

"Please stand back. I do not wish to injure you after you have been so kind to me."

Ernesto's eyes widened, and he squeezed his bulk closer to the wall.

Tāwera walked to the center of the open space, closed his eyes, and focused on his dragon. His shift was much smoother this time, and the pain was minimal. Elated, he opened his eyes and flapped his wings to lift into the air. Once airborne, he glanced down to check on Ernesto's position. He wanted to grab the bag containing his cheese and biscuits.

Ernesto remained frozen against the wall, his expression shocked, or perhaps it was admiration because his taniwha seemed way more solid than earlier. Tāwera hoped Nyree wouldn't be too angry with him if he promised not to show his dragon form again.

Tāwera darted closer and aimed his talons at the bag. Ernesto's eyes grew even rounder. Thankfully, Ernesto lifted the bag at the last moment. Tāwera scooped up the bag handles and lifted into the air. He arrowed from the ship, speeding as fast as possible because he hated to cause trouble for Nyree. His black form wasn't as showy as the red and green dragons his mother had told him she'd flown with before he was born, but in this case, he'd blend better with the mountains.

Shouts and screams came from one inflatable ferrying passengers from the shore to the ship.

Oh, no! This was bad. This was extremely bad, and he suspected Nyree might be very upset with him.

CHAPTER 8

Keep Your Hands to Yourself

Nyree heard the kerfuffle and immediately sensed this was dragon-related. The last of the passengers had wandered out of the store ten minutes ago. She balanced the till before placing the day's takings in a canvas bag. Hurriedly, she gave the shelves a quick scan and locked up. She stepped outside in time to see a black dragon fly over the hill and out of sight. Her mouth dropped open before she snapped her teeth together.

"Did you see that?" Carolyn asked.

Nyree had a split second to decide on which way to take the conversation. "See what?" she asked a beat later.

"It looked like a dragon, but I... No, that wasn't a blue shopping bag dangling from its talons." She rubbed her eyes and peered over Nyree's shoulder. She blinked again. "It's ridiculous. I didn't sleep well last night. Yes, that must be it."

"A dragon?" Nyree's brows rose as she pretended surprise and played dumb for Carolyn. Oh, yes. She'd seen a dragon all right. *Tāwera.* But the weird thing was that he was almost opaque. His black hide had stood out, as had the fact he was a dragon. Confusion filled Nyree along with burning questions. A trace of panic.

"Would you like me to lock the day's takings in the safe?"

Carolyn blinked again. "What?"

"The day's sales?"

"Oh, yes. Of course. You take the money and put it away. It looked as if you were busy today."

"Yes, I haven't restocked the store yet. I'll do it tomorrow morning if that's all right."

"That's fine," Carolyn said absently, her gaze on the white-capped mountain tops. "I obviously need more sleep."

Judging by the shouts and screams, others had seen Tāwera too. What had he been thinking? No, that wasn't fair. Tāwera hadn't shifted for hundreds of years. It was possible in his excitement he hadn't remembered to use stealth and remain out of sight of others.

Nyree checked her watch. There was another possibility. That might not have even been Tāwera, which raised fresh problems.

She hurried to the office and locked up the canvas bag before returning to her quarters. She'd hoped Tāwera would've returned, but her place was empty. Nyree stalked through the quiet rooms, restless yet part of her excited too.

She missed Tāwera, even though they'd only spent a short time together. *Crazy.* Pure idiocy on her part.

Nyree glanced out the window, her gaze lighting on the distant mountains. Perhaps this was a symptom of the coming full moon because if this was anything else, she was an idiot.

She'd barely rid herself of her Ari problems, so it was stupid to pursue any sort of interest in a cursed man.

"Gah!" Nyree threw her hands up in the air and decided to do something to quell her restlessness. She'd go for a walk, and maybe she'd meet up with Tāwera to put her worry to rest. Although why she worried about a man who'd been a successful warrior given the tattoos on his entire face—his *moko*.

Nyree changed her clothes, adding another layer more suitable for at least an hour of walking. She pulled on thick socks and her walking boots. She also grabbed her camera, packed water and two of her precious chocolate bars in her day pack before going in search of either Carolyn or Keith.

"I'm going for a walk," she said when she found Keith in the tiny lunchroom. "I don't know why, but I'm restless as if I need to stretch my legs." She glanced at her wristwatch. "I'll be back within three hours."

Keith smiled. "Thanks for letting us know. Carolyn says she's seeing things and is having a nap."

"Um, she told me she saw a dragon carrying a blue bag."

"That's what she told me," Keith said, shaking his head. "I didn't see a dragon, and I was standing on one of the old jetties, watching ferry operations. A big wave almost capsized the inflatable again this afternoon. There was lots of girlish screaming." He pulled a face. "I hope Caro is okay."

"Me too," Nyree said, feeling bad for Carolyn. "See you later."

Nyree set off up the hill. She dodged a wandering pair of king penguins before walking past the tiny white church and powering up the track to the top of the first rise. As always, she turned to enjoy the view over the bay and drag the clean air deep into her lungs. A humpback whale leaped from the water while another did a spy-hop. She grinned, never tiring of the panoramic beauty of this part of the world.

Today was cooler, and a brisk wind tugged at her braid. The cold never bothered her, and she was thriving in this far-flung island of South Georgia. Nyree continued striding along the ridge until the bay on the hill's far side became visible.

Something moved on the beach, attracting her attention, and when she focused, she let out a gasp. Tāwera, but it was his tattoos that snared her attention. They ran down his shoulder and torso and curved over one sculpted buttock.

He turned as if he sensed her watching him, and she waved. Her hand stilled in the wave position as she gaped at him.

Tāwera gestured for her to join him. She hadn't explored this beach before, preferring to go farther afield to guarantee privacy.

Nyree scrambled down the hill, and when Tāwera indicated she should walk farther along the crest, she discovered a path that zigzagged between the rocks. Five minutes later, she stepped onto the flat grassy area above the pebble-strewn beach. To her right, a broad glacier met the sea and glittered blue and white in the sunlight.

She located Tāwera, and her gaze zapped to his naked form. An unusual heat formed in her cheeks. "What happened to you? I can see you. Where are your clothes?"

"I left my clothes farther inland." He beamed at her. "The curse is loosening its hold."

"You're visible," Nyree repeated. While he wasn't handsome in the traditional sense, his features were strong with a stubborn jaw and a broad nose. His golden-brown eyes glinted with intelligence, and his body was a muscled work of art. Tāwera's skin was a deeper shade of brown than hers, and she positively itched to trace her fingers over the black whorls of his tattoos.

"Is something wrong? You're staring at me." Tāwera's eyes glowed with an inner fire, and it ignited an answering one in her.

"Um," she said, at a loss for words. The heat built in her cheeks. "You're very nice to look at." She groaned when he grinned at her.

"That wasn't me. I didn't say that."

"Which part do you like best?" He struck a pose, comfortable with his nudity.

Generally, she was relaxed with nakedness, but somehow, this seemed different. "I'm not answering that," she said in a firm voice. "Tell me what you did after we had breakfast together."

"I went exploring, walked around the buildings, and watched the big penguins with the yellow on their faces and the baby seals. Then I walked up the hill in the direction you suggested." He paused, his big shoulders rising and falling in a shrug.

Her gaze automatically followed the movement and slid over the delineated muscles of his abs. Unbidden, her attention slipped even lower, and a wash of heat filled her cheeks at his chuckle. She hurriedly ripped her gaze away to focus on the churning sea.

"You can look as much as you want," he assured her. It was simple to discern the amusement in his words. "It is so long since I have had the pleasure of a beautiful woman enjoying my body. Aroha..."

"Do you miss her?" Nyree asked, desperate to divert her thoughts.

Tāwera scowled. "My memories of her have faded, and I have wondered if I loved her as much as I thought. I recall a sweet girl, but her features escape me while my brother's face is distinct, especially my last view of him. My thoughts of Aroha are more nostalgic than full of love. Does this make me a bad man?"

"No." Nyree gulped at the rush of satisfaction his words brought and decided the safest course was to change the subject. "What happened while you were walking? Was that you who I saw flying across the bay?"

Tāwera winced. "I'm so sorry. That was an accident. I know better than to show myself in my taniwha form to those who don't understand. It won't happen again."

"It's all right as long as neither of us makes a habit of flying in front of others. What I want to know is what made you visible?"

"I am trying to tell you."

Nyree rolled her eyes and waited.

"I had a sudden yearning to fly through the mountains and explore. The full moon approaches." He shrugged those broad shoulders again, and his black hair shone under the sun. "Perhaps that is why... I found a private spot and disrobed. After I hid my clothes, I centered myself and pictured my taniwha. My shift was slow, much slower than I recall, and the pain. It was much worse than a *mere* to the head or a *taiaha* across the shoulders."

A flat stone club across the skull or a staff whack on the shoulders, Nyree interpreted as Tāwera continued speaking.

"I'd hate to get stuck between forms. When I was a child, my mother told me tales of this. The taniwha trapped between forms and ended up a monster. His *whānau* exiled him to a cave high in the mountains, and he had to scavenge to eat. When he started killing innocents who wandered too close, the tribe's warriors had to kill him. That was the last thing I wanted—to inflict this responsibility on you." Tāwera had lost his teasing, and his expression was somber as he met her gaze.

Nyree shuddered. "That sounds horrid. For his family to force him out. That must've been difficult for him."

"You have never heard of this occurrence?"

"No, but my mother and her brother always told me I must never try to stop shifting once I started the process. Never, under any circumstances, even if it meant a human spotted me. I guess that is why. They never told me if we got stuck, it was possible to become trapped halfway."

"Perhaps they did not wish to scare you," Tāwera said.

"Maybe. Carry on. You pushed through the pain and shifted to your taniwha form."

Tāwera darted a glance her way and seemed sheepish. "I'm frightened to tell you because I may have caused trouble."

"What did you do?"

"Once I shifted, I was still in pain. It wasn't as bad—not bad enough that a short flight was impossible. Before I knew it, I'd flown over the sea and discovered I'd lost the strength I took for granted. Trapped as I was, training was impossible, which caused me problems with fitness and weak muscles."

Nyree stared at him. "What happened?"

"The flight exhausted me. I knew I wouldn't make it to the shore before I fell into the sea. I saw the ship, and I crashed on their deck.

The ship wobbled with the force of my landing, which created a wave that took the humans by surprise."

"Did anyone get hurt?"

"I do not think so," Tāwera said.

"All right. What happened next?"

"I decided it would be best if I shifted back to my human form. This change was painful but not nearly as bad as the first one. My theory is," Tāwera said with a frown, "that the pain came because of my lack of shifting. The transformation from human to dragon and back is like a muscle that one must exercise to function correctly."

"That makes sense," Nyree said.

"Once I'd shifted, I explored the ship. Most people were ashore, and it was easy to wander at will. My curiosity," he said, his nose wrinkling and the corners of his eyes crinkling as he poked fun at himself. "It has always caused trouble for me. And food. The flight made my belly rumble with hunger, so I followed the aroma and discovered a huge bounty of food, waiting."

"A buffet," Nyree said in a faint voice. "What did you do?"

"I didn't know what most of the foods were, so I wandered around and tried the items. A man dressed in white came from a kitchen. He saw me eating. I must've startled him because he dropped his tray."

"He saw you?"

"Not at first. The man noticed the food lifting off the trays and disappearing as I placed it inside my mouth. Ernesto was with him and stayed to speak with me."

"Oh," Nyree said, her eyes wide. "What did you do next?"

"I was still starving. The humans kept adding platters of food, and I was in the way. Ernesto offered dessert and coffee. The men in white stared at me and became animated."

Nyree pictured the scene and laughed. She would've loved to witness their reactions as they'd watched food rise to an invisible mouth.

"The man dropped his trays and containers of *kai* on the floor. It was a waste of delicious *kai*. The food—Nyree, it was tasty."

"I'm sure it was, but I wonder if it was the food or the shift that made you visible. I could see you—an outline, at least. But right now, you look like a naked man. Normal, apart from the tattoos on your face. So, what happened with Ernesto?"

"Ernesto came to talk with me. I made him nervous, but he asked if I would like dessert and coffee. He said he would get it for me. I thanked him and finished eating. He was very polite when he suggested I left before the passengers returned. I told him that was fine. You may be right. The food seemed to help me become visible."

"All right. Ernesto seemed quite calm for a human. It's a wonder he didn't scream a warning about monsters."

"He knows I'm a dragon," Tāwera said. "He showed me the way to the forward deck. Ships differ from when I first saw them in the harbor at home."

"Yes, you've probably noticed many things have changed."

"I shifted on deck, took the bag Ernesto held up for me and flew back here to sleep on the beach. I have missed the sun and the breeze on my bare skin," Tāwera added. "Are you hungry?"

"Not right now. I might go for a flight. Would you like to come with me? We can take off from here and land where you left your clothes."

"That is a fine idea." Tāwera beamed. "We can eat after we shift back to human. Have one of those picnic things the *pākehā* men are so fond of having when they are working outdoors."

"Ah, I knew I brought those chocolate bars for a reason," Nyree said. "They can be a celebration. At least you've broken the curse and regained your previous abilities." She reached out her hand and squeezed a bulky biceps. "I can see and hear you. Your skin radiates heat."

"Is the beat of my heart audible?" Tāwera asked.

Nyree placed her palm on Tāwera's bare chest. The warmth from his skin raced up her fingers and down her arm. She became even more aware of him as a man. His strength. The differences between them. Her skin tingled, and she hurriedly lowered her lashes to screen her thoughts.

Tāwera noticed, however, attuned to her responses. "What's wrong?"

"I..." Her mind raced while she struggled to find an answer.

There wasn't one. After Ari, she should want to run in the opposite direction, but something about Tāwera called to her. He was kind and considered others, despite his warrior background. If Ari had been on the ship, he would've delighted in terrorizing the staff and passengers. Tāwera hadn't done that—not on purpose, at any rate.

"You make my skin buzz."

Nyree lifted her head to meet his gaze. "It's only because no one has touched you for so long."

"Or it might be moonlust," Tāwera conceded.

"You too?" Nyree whispered. "I was trying to ignore my taniwha."

"We don't have to do anything," Tāwera assured her. "We can fly in our taniwha forms, and that should suffice."

Nyree swallowed hard and decided she didn't want to hide her feelings from Tāwera. So far, she'd found him honest—refreshingly so—and she wanted to do the same for him. "I want to kiss you."

Tāwera stared at her for a long, extended moment, and his gaze dropped to her mouth. Then he shook himself. "We will go for a flight together and have our picnic. There is a beautiful spot near where I left my belongings."

Nyree's belly pulled tight, and it was in a good way rather than the fear she'd always experienced with Ari. He might not have been a taniwha, but he'd had a wide streak of meanness that had her treading carefully around him. With Tāwera, she didn't guard her words or try to gauge his mood before she spoke. Did he want to kiss her? Did he even know about kissing? Had they discussed this subject? Right now, her mind was a clean slate, and all she could think of was him and sex.

Fast and furious sex. Slow and tender. A shudder worked through Nyree.

Good grief. The tug of the moon was worse some months, more intense and full-on, but the way her nerves jumped and sparked right now, this time might be on another level. Luckily, he hadn't kissed her because she feared her control might snap at the first physical contact.

"I'd love to fly with you," she said, and this was an understatement.

Never had she flown with a male taniwha unrelated to her. "We need to take care, though. We must try to escape attention. Visibility is excellent today."

"You shift. I have something to collect before I take off." Tāwera strode toward a shady area before he'd even finished speaking.

Her gaze went straight to the tattoos winding down the right side of his torso, over his buttock and down his thigh. She imagined licking the lines with her tongue, and heat shot through her, leaving her breathless with need. She released a tiny moan and forced herself to glance away.

Time to shift. Right.

Nyree yanked off her clothes, despite the air of self-consciousness that swept her. She folded her clothes and crouched to place them inside her daypack. Once she'd secured her boots to the outside of her pack, and she was confident she wouldn't drop or lose them en route, she rose and stepped back, ready to shift. A prickle at her back told her Tāwera was watching her as closely as she'd studied him. She didn't make the mistake of sneaking a glance in his direction. This situation was complicated enough already.

"Ready?" Tāwera asked.

"Yes." Nyree proved it by backing up farther and shifting to her taniwha. Her transformation was fast and pain-free. She snatched up her pack in her right talon and rose upward. Once airborne, she hovered to wait for Tāwera. His shift was sluggish, and he grunted, which told her the morph from human to a dragon was still uncomfortable. She must ask him if the change had always proved difficult. Long moments later, Tāwera rose, the flap of his wings slower than her own. It was noticeable he was still experiencing difficulties after escaping the stone curse.

Nyree let Tāwera set the pace. She followed, scrutinizing him closely and a little curious about the blue bag he carried. His breathing soon became labored, and worry pulsed to life in her. He hadn't flown for hundreds of years and should approach this new lease of life with caution. Nyree scanned their surroundings and spotted the cruise ship leaving the bay.

She released a quick burst of flame to attract Tāwera's attention. *"What is it?"*

Tāwera's voice flowed through her mind, startling her so much she forgot to flap her wings. Normally, she could only communicate with family and those of related blood. She plummeted before she self-corrected. *"The ship is leaving. We must hurry in case they spot us. Fly lower to skim the peaks and stay away from those with snow. We are more visible against the white mountainside."*

"The place where I took off from is over the mountain ahead of us."

Nyree kept pace with him, relieved when they flew into a valley and out of sight of anyone at sea. Tāwera flew deep into the valley and landed near a rushing mountain stream. There were no trees, but moss and lichen covered the rocks and other mystery herbaceous plants. It was a beautiful spot, and it probably wasn't a well-thought-out idea on her part to be alone here with an enticing man such as Tāwera.

Nyree shifted, and Tāwera followed suit. Once again, her transformation was much faster than his. A grunt escaped him, and he pressed his hands to his knees, panting.

Nyree stepped closer. "Can I help?"

Tāwera gasped and sucked in a huge breath as he straightened. He grinned at her. "The shifts are becoming easier each time. Eating seems to help."

"I have a chocolate bar," Nyree said, turning away.

"Ernesto gave me food," Tāwera said.

"What?" Nyree turned back to Tāwera and caught him checking out her arse. His gaze lifted to her breasts, and she had to fight to stop raising her hands to cover them.

"Don't hide. I enjoy looking at you. In clothes and without," he added, and then he closed his eyes in an attempted and exaggerated wink.

The familiar heat roared through her, and it was her turn to suck in a steadying breath. She couldn't even blame the approach of the full moon for the lust that roared through her. It was Tāwera. He wasn't only pleasant to look at, but she genuinely liked him. His personality. How on earth was she going to keep her hands to herself?

CHAPTER 9

Mountain Picnic

Tāwera dragged in air, fighting to remain upright while focusing on the womanly fragrance riding the air. His muscles cried out, screaming abuse with the fractured signals shooting upward to his shoulders, his neck to the back of his head. It was Nyree's clean, green scent that shredded his concentration and helped to push away the pain. He smiled even though it hurt. Everything throbbed, but he didn't care. The soreness meant he was alive and no longer in hibernation or whatever the curse had done to him.

He stared at Nyree, taking in her slender beauty. Muscles rippled under her skin, yet she was feminine.

"It would please me to kiss you," he whispered. "I want that very much, but first, we should eat."

He picked up the bag Ernesto had given him and pulled out the box. "Let's sit over there on the flat rock. It's out of the wind and should be pleasant in the sun. When I get cold, the aching in my bones is worse."

"That's interesting. You can have a hot shower when we get back." She pulled on a pair of leggings and a shirt before picking her way across the uneven ground strewn with rocks. A pebble skittered away when she kicked it with her toe.

"I prefer you without clothes," Tāwera said, setting the box on the rock. "And I'm looking forward to the kiss you offered me."

Nyree's mouth opened and closed, reminding him of an eel fished from the river.

He grinned as he retrieved his cloak and other garments, his pain receding and allowing him to function better. "Sit here," he said, patting the rock. After donning his *piupiu* since his naked state bothered Nyree, he opened the food box, and the powerful aroma of aged cheddar reached him. Ernesto had done him proud with tasty cheese, biscuits, and fruit. Tāwera unpacked the items on the small bendy trays Ernesto had included. They were like plates but appeared constructed of tough paper.

"What are these?" He held up several round things, his *piupiu* swishing around his legs as he moved.

Nyree leaned closer and sniffed. "*Mmm.* Chocolate truffles.

They're delicious and usually eaten with a cup of strong coffee to counteract the sweetness."

Tāwera peered inside his box of treats. "There is no coffee." He pulled out a bottle. "Is this water?"

"Yes, and it's from France by the looks of the label. That will work perfectly with the feast you've provided."

"I'm not sure of the identity of some of these things," he confessed.

Nyree grinned, and her animated expression warmed him through. His painfully tense muscles released from the cramp, causing him discomfort. Making Nyree happy boosted his mood.

"The items on this plate are different French cheeses. This one is blue cheese. It tastes strong. I'm not sure if you'll enjoy it or not. This is a cheddar. A brie. If I had to guess, this one is a type of goat cheese. This plate contains pieces of French bread and crackers. The fruit on this plate—you have grapes, sliced apple and pear, and mandarin segments. A handful of nuts. You even have pickle or relish. Ernesto has given you a feast."

"He wanted to get rid of me," Tāwera stated.

"Perhaps," Nyree said with a giggle.

Tāwera's stomach let out a grumble. "What should we try first?"

"Try the cheddar. I'm sure you'll like that. Have you had cheese before?" As she spoke, Nyree pulled a white object from her pack.

"What's that?" Tāwera had never seen an object such as this.

"It's my Swiss army knife. I take it everywhere with me. The blades of the knife fold out and slip back when you're finished using them."

He watched Nyree slice the cheese with the sharp blade. She passed the cheese and bread to him before slicing the other cheeses. She spread a reddish-brown paste on the bread and placed a slice of cheese on the top before sitting back to study the view and take a bite.

"This is beautiful," she said. "A feast, splendid company, and a spectacular panorama."

Tāwera reached for a grape and a piece of the pungent blue cheese. He nibbled a corner.

"Do you like that?"

"Yes, it tastes different from anything I've tried, but it is interesting," he said, eating with more enthusiasm. He rolled his neck and shoulders. "Eating makes the deepest muscle pains recede."

Nyree reached for nuts and fruit. "I'm glad you're feeling better and that the symptoms of the curse are passing, but I'm not sure how to explain your presence. I doubt Carolyn and Keith will understand the abrupt appearance of a tattooed man."

Tāwera lounged back on the sand, his gaze on two white-and-black birds flying past their vantage point. Their presence didn't bother the birds. As he watched, more appeared, flying lazily on the air currents and heading toward the water.

"The people I've seen here don't have tattoos," Tāwera said.

SHELLEY MUNRO

"You don't have a *moko* on your chin. Are the old traditions no longer followed?"

Nyree wrinkled her nose. "Tattoos fell out of fashion. I suspect the missionaries had a part to play in this since, from what I've read of our history, they disapproved of tattoos."

"The missionaries I knew had very straight minds."

Nyree frowned, then her expression cleared. "Oh, you mean they had narrow minds."

He nodded. "They didn't like people having fun."

"There was a time when most people thought those with tattoos were villains and untrustworthy."

Tāwera jerked upright. "You can trust me." Indignation filled his taut body.

"Wait. I'm doing a poor job of explaining. In the past, many people felt this way. In the last ten to twenty years, tattoos have become acceptable. It's a way of expressing individuality. Many famous men and women—actors, singers, and sports stars—get tattoos and the young people follow their lead. At home, many Māori are turning to the old ways. It's not so unusual to see men with full facial tattoos like yours and women with standing within their tribe might have chin *moko*."

"I have missed much."

"It's true the curse shut you away, but it has also given you an opportunity to embrace the future."

"Can you show me how to use your machines? Two of the men

in white pointed their machines at me. What happens when they do that?"

Nyree gasped. "Oh, no. They took photos?"

"What is a photo?"

"Remember I showed you the images on my computer? Those are photos. I can take them with my phone or with my camera."

Tāwera nodded, but Nyree's words still confused him.

She patted his arm as if she read his mind and understood. "I'll show you once we get back. Try not to let them photograph you again."

His brows lifted. "I should blow fire at them?"

"No! It's even more important these days to keep our true identities secret. There are people out there—governments—who would capture us and use us in ways I don't even want to imagine." Nyree shuddered.

"They could take down a mighty taniwha?" he scoffed, his disdain clear. Nothing was more powerful than a dragon.

"That might have been true once. The local people feared and revered the taniwha. There was mutual respect. When we return, I'll introduce you to the internet. I might download a book on world history for you to read. Are your reading skills as good as your verbal?"

"I can read, but I am slow."

"That's all right. You need to learn as much as you can before returning to New Zealand. Reading books will help you prepare for the modern world. Now back to Keith and Carolyn. We must hide you because they'd have to report you to their boss. That would raise even more questions."

"I can find a place to hide, but when the cruise ships come, I can walk in the open."

"Yes, that should work. You can sneak into my quarters at night. The thing is to look confident as if you belong. That way, you'll receive fewer questions."

"I can do this." Tāwera reached for more cheese. "We do not have another alternative. I am stuck here at present." He crunched down on a piece of French bread and cheese and immediately spat it out. "Ugh!"

"I'm not a fan of the goat cheese either. We won't eat that one."

Once they'd demolished their feast, they relaxed in the sun until Nyree checked her watch and said it was time to return, otherwise Keith and Carolyn would worry. She stood and slapped the dust from her backside.

Tāwera stood too. "First, we will have our kiss because your soft lips entice me."

"Kissing involves more than the pressing of lips. There is a technique." Nyree drew in a sharp breath, and a hint of pink crept up her neck. "Excellent. I sound like a prissy maiden aunt."

"There is more?" Tāwera regarded her with a curious expression, his gaze following the path of the delightful pink as it traveled upward to her cheeks. "Show me."

Before Nyree could comment—the flustered tangle of her tongue prevented an immediate reply—he stepped closer and grasped her shoulders with gentle fingers. He lowered his lips to hers, the movement a whisper of pleasure. *Oh, boy.* Tāwera knew precisely what a kiss was and how to give a great one. She gripped his shoulders and held tight as he teased her mouth. At first, the kiss was slow with an inherent tenderness, but gradually Tāwera deepened the contact, using his tongue and teeth to perfect effect. He licked and nibbled, and pressure built inside Nyree's chest. The emotion emerged in a heartfelt groan. Tāwera had been holding back on her.

She'd tried not to think about him and sex, but he'd torn down the flimsy barrier she'd erected with one exceptional kiss. It made her curious about what he'd be like as a lover. He tugged her closer, fitting their bodies together. Every feminine part of her rejoiced at the contact. He was hard everywhere. His chest. His shoulders. His cock.

Aghast at her thoughts when she'd only escaped her last relationship—a toxic one—with the help of her friends, she yanked from his embrace, each breath seesawing up her throat.

Tāwera stilled, and she'd bet his watchful brown gaze saw more than he should, more than she was comfortable with him seeing. They held a stare for a long, tension-filled moment.

Tāwera broke the silence first. "Did I do something wrong?"

"No." The word emerged with a snap, and she winced.

He cocked his head, reminding her of an inquisitive *pīwakawaka*, the fantail that flicked through the forest and long grasses hunting bugs on the wing.

Nyree sighed. It wasn't fair to cast any blame for her confusion on him. This was all her. "I..." she started and sighed again. "I'm sorry."

"Did you not enjoy my kiss?"

Nyree gaped at the arrogant tilt of his chin, the smug male glint in those ever-changing brown eyes of his. Right now, they reminded her of an expensive Scottish whisky.

"Nyree?"

The verbal prod had Nyree shaking herself. "I loved your kiss. Too much. I liked it too much, and that's a problem, especially with the coming of the full moon. I don't trust myself, and I shouldn't be looking at any man, not after my disastrous relationship with Ari."

"It wasn't your fault."

Nyree shrugged, impatience surging through her. "I should take half the blame. I should've walked away earlier or fought back. Stood up for myself."

"Protecting others is never wrong," Tāwera said.

At his words, tears formed in her eyes, and she blinked hard to keep them at bay.

"What if I want to kiss you again?" Tāwera said. That sexy glint in those whisky eyes of his hinted that he wanted way more than a kiss.

A slippery slope, for sure.

"It wouldn't be right," she said and bent to pick up her pack. "I need to go before Carolyn and Keith worry about me."

"What should I do?"

Nyree hated the idea of making him sleep outside. That didn't seem fair. "I'll try to find you clothes to help you to blend, and we might need to experiment with makeup because your *moko* is so distinctive. One good thing to come from my relationship with Ari. I became an expert with makeup. We'll work out a basic disguise. Maybe one or two different ones."

"Thank you, Nyree. I owe you much."

"You're welcome." He didn't owe her a thing. If anything, he was helping her, giving her someone to talk to, and ease her loneliness. A fellow taniwha, which was something she'd never have with Ari. "I'll pack the leftover food in my daypack. We can have it for supper tonight."

"Ernesto was a most generous man."

"He wanted to avoid pandemonium in his restaurant and worked out that food was a way to make you cooperate."

Tāwera chuckled. "This is true."

They cleaned up together, making sure to leave no trash behind in the pristine environment. Once they were ready to depart, they lifted off.

"What will you do for the full moon? You have plans?" Tāwera asked.

Nyree startled even as she marveled at the ability they had to communicate. No one she knew connected in this manner. Only family members or mates—shock punched through her at this thought.

She'd never considered this angle, but now her mind seized on it and rejected the information. Tāwera might have the ability to speak to others, but...

"Can you hear me?"

"I was thinking." Boy, was she ever. She needed to send another message to Manu, and this one would be harder to write, but she suspected Manu and his wife might have answers for her. *"I'd intended to sneak out at night and go flying. Probably for the nights leading up to the full moon and for one night afterward. For me, once the moon wanes, I no longer experience the pull. I know this isn't the same for all taniwha, but it seems true for me."*

"For me, as well. Some men in my mother's family used to sleep outdoors during the height of the full moon. When they slept deep in the mountains, they did not have to worry about others witnessing their flights or expecting them to return."

"I could go camping. That is what we call sleeping outside now."

"We."

"We could go camping. I have a tent and attended the survival camp training. That is a brilliant idea because we wouldn't have

to sneak around. It will depend if there is a cruise ship in during the day. It will be even busier soon with cruise ships coming in the morning and the afternoon. Grytviken is a popular port because of its association with Shackleton."

"Tell me about this, Shackleton. I wish to know the history."

Nyree spent the rest of the short flight telling Tāwera about the English explorer who spent much time in Antarctica and about his ill-fated voyage where he saved his men from certain death. *"I'm still reading about the voyages he took, but I know he spent some time in New Zealand.* Aotearoa," she added since this name was more familiar to Tāwera. *"Shackleton's wife agreed to have him buried in the cemetery here because he loved this region so much. I usually walk from down here."*

Tāwera landed at her side and shifted. They dressed in silence.

"I thought I might vanish again," Tāwera said, glancing at his arm. "I do not think that will happen."

"It doesn't matter. We'll work out something. I should've thought of clothes for you before, but you didn't need them as much when you were invisible. We'll search the wardrobes in the spare rooms for clothes. I'm certain I saw some on the hangers."

"No one will see me. I will sneak."

"Most of the scientists are away at the glacier, and the contractors are eradicating noxious plants at the far end of the island. It's tomorrow night we must worry because everyone is coming back then. Keith mentioned they usually have a party when everyone is here."

Tāwera slipped an arm around her waist and drew her close. "Don't worry. We will make this work." And then he kissed her.

CHAPTER 10

Out of Control

Three days later, Nyree was still thinking about their kiss and how her knees had buckled. She'd participated in the kiss with too much eagerness.

She hadn't intended to kiss him again or let him touch her at all. He'd taken her unawares, and the gleam in those sexy eyes of his had told her he'd known what he wanted.

It seemed men had changed little across the generations.

"Nyree!" The sharp note in Carolyn's voice told Nyree this wasn't the first time Carolyn had tried to grab her attention.

"I'm sorry." Nyree shoved the sexy Tāwera from her mind to focus on right now—the museum where she and Carolyn had met this morning and the day's schedule. She gripped her duster a little tighter. Nyree loved this job, and she'd hate to put it in jeopardy. It was bad enough that she was hiding Tāwera. She didn't want Keith or Carolyn to brand her as unreliable.

"I want you to take the tours today," Carolyn said. "I have a sore throat, and I'm not feeling well. A woman on the tour three days ago coughed and spluttered all over me."

"Carolyn, why don't you go back to bed and catch a couple of hours of sleep?" Now that she studied Carolyn, her paleness and the shadows under her eyes were noticeable. "I can take care of the preliminary stuff. I'll take the morning tour and open the shop once I've finished. It's more important for you to rest and get better."

"That's what I told her," Keith said, appearing behind Carolyn. "My wife is very stubborn."

"I can cope with this, and if I run into problems, Keith will be around. Please, Carolyn, rest. The shadows under your eyes show your restless night."

"She lay awake half the night," Keith said. "Love, Nyree is right. You'll get better faster if you relax now. Besides, we don't want Nyree or the scientists to get sick."

Carolyn retreated to their quarters, still arguing, but Keith mouthed a silent thank you over his shoulder as he escorted his wife away.

Nyree hustled to the shop and wished she'd taken the time to restock the previous day. She glanced around for Tāwera. When she couldn't see him, she silently hailed him.

To her surprise, he answered her telepathically.

"You called?" Tāwera asked, his tone teasing.

She frowned even as she thrilled at the intimate rumble of his voice curling into her mind. Manu still hadn't replied, and this was yet another thing to communicate to her tribal leader. He'd be sick of her by the time she finished this assignment.

She'd noted Tāwera had picked up more modern slang from his reading. At present, he was devouring detective novels and books detailing the history of New Zealand.

"If you're not busy, could you help me stock the shelves at the shop? I should've done it yesterday evening, but exhaustion got the better of me. Carolyn is sick, and Keith has escorted her back to their quarters."

"I was walking on the beach. The cruise ship staff have come ashore already, so I don't stand out. They think I'm a scientist, and the scientists think I'm one of the crew."

"Thanks," Nyree said.

She started dragging boxes of T-shirts from the storage room.

"I'll take those," Tāwera said, appearing in the doorway. "You bring the lighter stuff. Don't argue. I know you're strong, but this will be faster."

With practiced ease, they refilled the shelves and readied the store for the incoming passengers.

"I'm taking the tours, and I'll open the shop once I finish," she said.

"Can I take your tour?"

"Yes, but you'll be sick of listening to my voice soon."

"Never." He leaned closer and kissed her cheek, retreating before her mind kicked into gear. His decadent soapy scent and a hint of the green pine that clung to his skin filled her nostrils and tormented her because she wanted to inhale more.

Disappointment surged through her. A problem. For her, at least. She was falling for Tāwera in a big way. It didn't help that it was the full moon tomorrow night, and every part of her skin sizzled with awareness. If she couldn't fly tonight, her vibrator would have to make an appearance, and she imagined that'd cause embarrassing questions because Tāwera's hearing was even better than hers.

She locked the store and went to meet the first boat heading ashore. This one contained passengers rather than staff or guides because the occupants wore the distinctive bright orange jackets the cruise company gave their passengers. The wind had changed direction, and she got a hit of penguin poo. It'd never be a designer perfume, but it was growing on her. She stalked over to the arrival point and pasted a smile in place.

Slowly, the passengers drifted to a stop, and Nyree introduced herself. "Good morning. My name is Nyree. Welcome to Grytviken. I'll give you the quick down-low on the things you can do during your visit, then you're free to use your time however you wish. You've probably already noticed the cemetery. There, you'll find Shackleton's grave, along with those of sealers and soldiers. If you head in this direction, you'll come to the Grytviken church. Feel free to go inside. I'll be leading a tour in exactly one hour, which will leave from outside the post office. I'll give you an overview of the whaling history and take you around the station here."

"Where is the post office?" A blonde girl bounced on her toes, enthusiasm shining on her round face. Her ponytail jerked from side to side, and Nyree hid her smile.

"If you walk past this shed, you'll see the sign. You'll find the museum near there too. The shop will be closed during the tour, so if you want to mail a letter or purchase a T-shirt, do it before the tour or afterward. The tour goes for around half an hour. Do you have questions? No?" Nyree smiled. "Remember, the tour will start at eleven prompt. I'll go through the island's history, and you'll hear a lot about the whaling industry. Enjoy Grytviken."

The passengers dispersed, and Nyree hustled to the shop. Tāwera loitered outside. He'd dressed in black jeans, a black T-shirt advertising a brewpub in Los Angeles, and a pair of old gumboots. He carried an orange jacket over his arm and wore a black cap.

"Where did you get the jacket?"

"I acquired it from the scientists. I overheard them discussing cleaning out an old building to make way for new arrivals. The

143

man in charge told them to heap all the unwanted clothing together, and he'd get rid of it. I grabbed several items to make me blend."

"Excellent thinking. We were lucky to find jeans to fit you. Oops, looks like a line is forming. I'd better open up before they break down the doors."

Tāwera kept pace with her. "They would do that?" he asked, his brows drawn together.

"It's a figure of speech," Nyree explained. "Go. Eavesdrop on our visitors. You'll hear accents from different parts of the world. It will help you learn to fit in with different people."

"I thought I would help you."

"You've already done that by stocking the shelves, and I'd love your aid later. Right now, I think you'll learn more by listening to different men and women. Just don't flirt with the women," she added with a wink.

"I only wish to flirt with you." He leaned closer. "Your lips are perfect for kissing."

Nyree's mouth dropped open, and she stared at him. "Where did you learn that?"

Tāwera grinned—a full-out smile that took him from handsome to mouthwateringly sexy. "I've been listening to the scientists."

"The scientists are talking about me?"

"Yes, but they said nothing to make me hit them. They were polite and behaved as if their mother was present." Tāwera winked at her, but he hadn't quite got the hang of it. Both of his eyes flicked closed before he opened them, and a hint of mischief peeked back at her.

Her heart beat in double-time, and she bit back a sigh at his unconscious charm. Nyree's gaze dropped to his mouth, and as she did this, his lips quirked upward. Her gaze jumped to his. *Caught in the act.* Even as her cheeks heated, she made a shooing motion with her hands and ushered him away. "Listen to the new arrivals. The scientists are weird. You want to learn from a wide variety of people, and this is the perfect way for you to study modern behavior. No flirting. No drawing attention to yourself. This means if someone upsets you, don't react. You must walk away, but you can tell me about them later, and we can swear up a storm together."

"We will gosh-golly them?"

Nyree spluttered. "Where did you learn those words?"

"From the missionaries."

"Oh." It was a struggle not to laugh, but she didn't want to hurt his feelings. "I'll teach you a modern curse later—one you can insert into a relevant conversation so you'll fit in better."

Tāwera nodded, eagerness in him now.

"If you come across something you don't understand, save your questions until we're in private."

Tāwera nodded a second time and strode away. Nyree spared a second to study his rear end before she plucked a shop keys from her pocket.

"Is he your boyfriend?" the blonde from earlier asked.

Nyree jumped. Despite her taniwha senses, she hadn't heard the girl's approach.

"Sorry, I didn't mean to scare you. That man is fine. His facial tattoos are distinctive. He's from New Zealand, right? I visited there last year and read lots of history before I arrived."

"Yes," Nyree said. "Come in and browse. Let me get the lights."

The next hour was the busiest she'd ever been, and shutting the shop to start her tour took so long, she ended up five minutes late.

"I'm so sorry," Nyree said. "Let's move. Back in the early 1900s, whaling started here in Grytviken. See that bay out there? It's not huge, but there were so many whales that the men hunting them didn't need to leave this area."

Nyree led the group around the rusty machinery and over the ramp where the whalers dragged the massive mammals up for butchering. She scanned the faces of the men and women who followed her around the small settlement. Most of the guests listened attentively to her spiel and took photos. Tāwera remained on the outskirts, and whenever he caught her gaze, he gave his version of a wink, charming her.

Her skin heated, and her belly tightened. Nyree breathed carefully and tried to focus on her tour. At the end of half an hour, she was pleased to finish because her mind hadn't been on the job. Tāwera kept intruding, and each time she spotted him, she thought of the coming full moon.

She was heading straight to her bedroom during her lunch break. Today, they had a narrow window between cruise ships, and she intended to take full advantage of the respite. Never mind food. She'd whip out her vibrator. Too bad if Tāwera heard. She'd explain this to him in upfront detail. Given the sizzle of her skin and her swollen sex, she'd self-combust if she didn't have an orgasm or two to release the sexual pressure taking her body by storm.

An hour later, Nyree stalked to her quarters, and Tāwera trotted beside her. They dodged a seal and two Gentoo penguins. A brown skua wheeled overhead, letting out a predatory squawk that had the black-and-white penguins diving for cover. Now the ship had left, leaving the settlement peaceful. However, the tempest that raged within her had her balanced on a knife-edge.

"Why are you walking so fast?" Tāwera asked.

"I have something I need to do," Nyree said, tension leaking into her voice.

"Can I help with something?"

"No. *No.*" And if she told herself that enough, she might come to believe this. Nyree reached the doorway of her place and unlocked it. She flung the door open and stepped inside. "I'm feeling the effects of moonlust. I am going to my room and getting out my vibrator to take off the edge before I do something crazy."

"What's a vibrator?"

"*Huh,*" Nyree muttered, closing her eyes and praying for

patience. "I'll explain everything later." Nyree marched directly to her bedroom and slammed the door behind her. Her skin warmed and tingled while every nerve ending in her body pulsated.

She yanked off her boots and dropped them haphazardly on the floor. One. Two. She tossed her socks on top and rapidly stripped off the rest of her clothes. The cooler air caused her nipples to pucker and pull tight. She dragged in a deep breath, and a groan squeezed past her lips. Every breath smelled of Tāwera.

Before she thought better of the action, she marched to the doorway and flung open the door. Tāwera stood there, his fist raised as if he'd intended to knock. Nyree grabbed his biceps and dragged him inside her room. He looked startled and unsure for an instant until she began tearing at his clothes.

He tugged at his T-shirt when she tried to yank it over his head. "What are you doing?"

Nyree didn't dissemble. "It's moonlust. I have to work this afternoon, but I can't concentrate. I don't have time to go for a flight. I was going to get out my vibrator, but I can smell you." Nyree stared at her feet, unable to keep talking without extreme discomfort.

"What should I do?" Tāwera asked.

"I don't want you to do anything," she snapped, angry at herself and her heritage. "I'm sorry. Go. I'm getting my vibrator out of the drawer. I'll get myself off so I can calm down and go back to work." She sniffed. "Why is this happening now? I've never reacted this strongly at a full moon."

"Nyree," Tāwera whispered. He walked to the door and didn't leave. Instead, he shut it and returned to her side. He tugged her against her chest and embraced her. For an instant, she held herself stiffly, then the fight went out of her. Tāwera kissed her cheek and followed this with another kiss closer to her mouth.

She twisted away, her heart beating so fast she wondered if it might burst from her body.

"Let me help you," Tāwera said, his gaze meeting hers. "My moonlust isn't as bad as yours, but I can still help."

"No, you don't have to," Nyree said. "I have my vibrator. Leave me on my own, and I'll take care of the problem myself."

Tāwera screwed up his nose, and she couldn't decide if his reaction was good or bad. "Please, Nyree. What is a vibrator?"

He wanted to know. She'd show him.

Nyree stomped to the rickety veneer nightstand. Years of use had taken their toll on the cheap piece of furniture. She'd found a book of the perfect size to keep the cabinet level. She ripped open the top drawer and tugged so hard, the contents flew out, scattering like a colorful explosion of confetti. Hair ties. Two filmy scarves. Tampons. Her electric blue vibrator.

"*Gah!*" Nyree shouted.

Tāwera—sensible man—took one giant step back and stared at her and the contents of her drawer with wide brown eyes.

When he said nothing, Nyree sniffed and plucked her vibrator off the floor. She stomped to the compact bathroom and gave it a wash. Although she'd cleaned her accommodation thoroughly on her arrival, one couldn't be too careful with hygiene.

On her return, she found Tāwera had picked up the fallen items and stacked them neatly inside the drawer.

He held up a tampon and turned it over. "What is this?"

"A tampon," Nyree snapped, refusing to allow embarrassment to take control. "For the time of the month when I bleed."

He frowned and glanced from her to the tampon. "How does it work? Aroha used a special moss. Does this contain something for the pain?" He inspected it from all angles.

His matter-of-fact acceptance eased some of her angst. "The tampon comprises special material. It goes inside me and swells. I change it as necessary. If I get cramps, I'll take a painkiller."

"Do you go to a special place with the other women?"

Her lip curled. "A place of banishment?" Her words carried a distinct bite.

"No!" He sounded shocked. "We never banished our women. They went to rest and do as much or little as they wanted. It was their time of celebration, and if they bled for the first time, it was extra joyful with gifts and *waiata*."

"They sang songs because they'd started their period?"

"Yes. This was a time of acknowledging the connection between the people and the land, the common ground with our ancestors."

"*Huh,*" Nyree said. "That sounds much nicer than what

happens now. We seldom discuss a woman's time of the month."

"What is that? It looks like a weird *ure*." At her frown, he gestured at his cock.

"Yes, that is exactly what it is. It is a fake cock that a woman can use to pleasure herself if she does not have a man."

When he continued to look puzzled, Nyree handed over the vibrator. It looked small in his big hands. "You place this inside you?"

"Yes." Now she sounded defensive. "I can't get pregnant with a vibrator."

"You don't want children?" His gaze was intent as he asked this.

"Yes, I'd like to have babies, but not right now."

"You cannot choose when to have *tamariki*," he said.

"These days, you can. I take a pill each day to stop a child from forming. And we're finished with this discussion." She grabbed the vibrator from Tāwera and somehow hit the start button before she had control of it. It sprang to life with a loud buzz.

"*Gosh-golly!*" Tāwera let out a manly shout and released the vibrator. "It moved," he said in horror, his eyes big rounds in his pale face.

"It does that. Out. Time's a-wastin'. I need to be back at the store in time for the next cruise ship."

When Tāwera didn't move, Nyree shrugged. She could do this with him in the room. If she shocked him enough, he'd leave anyway. A shudder went through her, arousal a riptide that left not one inch of her skin untouched. She dropped to the bed and splayed her legs, uncaring of what Tāwera might think. She closed her eyes, desperate for release.

Nyree slipped the vibrator inside her, turning up the power and manipulating the fake penis to hit her G-spot. She dragged it out, her pace slow and steady, a groan working free as she massaged her clit at the same time.

A soft touch at her breast had her eyes flying open.

"Let me," Tāwera said, his eyes darker than usual.

Nyree's breath caught. His irises were almost black, and she got the sense she was staring straight into the heart of his taniwha. Without breaking their visual connection, he stroked the side of her breast. A shiver ran through her, down her torso, and straight to her sex. A jab of pleasure resounded back, and her eyes drifted closed.

Tāwera settled on the bed beside her, his big, callused hands caressing and stroking her breasts, her nipples. He seemed to understand what she wanted instinctively. He grounded her with his firm touch. His pinches. The way he rolled her nipple between finger and thumb. His hand lifted, and she moaned in protest at the loss of contact.

Now that Tāwera had touched her, she craved more. Much more, and she was aware of the ticking clock. He settled beside her, a muscular, warm and naked body.

"Let me love you," he whispered against her ear.

"But we're friends. Your camaraderie is important to me." That was the truth, but she experienced an extra something that wasn't solely friendship. This growing emotion was going to cause trouble for her. She knew this, but at this moment, she didn't care.

"I will always be your loyal friend," he said. "Always."

She slid the vibrator from her needy body, turned it off, and set it aside. Her flesh pulsed, and she stirred restlessly, urgency thrumming through her body.

Tāwera didn't speak, but Nyree didn't care. An action man—that is what she needed at this moment. Tāwera didn't disappoint her. He cupped her breasts and settled between her legs. His mouth landed on hers, and as he pushed into her hot flesh, his pace unhurried, she started to come. Her body twitched. Bliss poured from her clit and rushed up to her chest and down to her toes. She pulsed around his cock as he thrust. The joy and excitement didn't fade or tail off.

Instead, she exploded into a second orgasm even more powerful than the first. Nyree gripped Tāwera's broad shoulders and clung.

"Nyree." Her name was a masculine rumble of satisfaction.

Nyree bit his shoulder, astounded and amazed, a little shocked at her reaction to Tāwera. Tāwera issued a guttural groan and increased the pace of his strokes. Without warning, he stilled, embedded deep in her while tiny spasms continued to dart enjoyment through her.

"Are you all right?" Tāwera whispered.

His first thoughts, first words were of concern for her. His example of caring made her fiercely glad she'd kicked Ari to the curb and left New Zealand to regather her mental strength.

"I'm perfect," Nyree whispered, peppering his broad shoulders with kisses in a show of appreciation. She relaxed against his body, at peace for the first time in ages. Yet, a small part of her knew she'd made a mistake because Tāwera differed from modern-day men.

"Thank you for sharing your moonlust with me," Tāwera murmured against her neck. "I'd forgotten how it is to hold a beautiful woman in my arms."

And bull's eye. A few kind and tender words and she turned to mush.

"I should have a quick shower and go back to work."

"You have not eaten."

"That wasn't the appetite I needed sating," Nyree said, her tone dry. "I'll be fine." She forced herself to pull from Tāwera's embrace, the sexual release leaving her level and less volatile. "I should thank you."

"It was my pleasure. Any time." Tāwera relaxed his grip and let her stand. "I am at your disposal. All you need to do is ask."

That was precisely what worried her. Another man in her life would bring complications she didn't need.

CHAPTER 11

The Email

Nyree plunged into work for the afternoon, too busy to think about what had happened with Tāwera. During the odd spare moment, she forced herself to ponder what she might do once the summer ended. Her job with George Taniwha & Sons challenged her, and she enjoyed her workmates and their camaraderie. It had been the one thing she'd kept, despite Ari's unreasonable demands. Even though he'd coveted the money she earned, more recently, he'd wanted her to stay at home and start a family.

A dodged bullet.

Customers tromped into the store and kept her busy with post office duties. She sold dozens of stamps for postage to far-flung corners of the world. After her tour, which Tāwera attended again, she stocked up, ready for the following day before heading home.

"My tattoos make me stand out," he said when they met in her kitchen.

"Perhaps a touch of makeup might disguise them," Nyree suggested and opened the fridge to study the contents. If she focused hard, she wouldn't try to drag his scent of green and nature and soap deep into her lungs.

"Would it mean I would fit in better?"

"Yes. You might need to cut your hair or wear it in a different style too."

"I will think on this. What will we eat for dinner?"

"The cooks on the cruise ship gave us a supply of fresh vegetables. Keith said he has a bag for me. I'll collect it, and we'll work out what to have once I see the bounty."

"I wish to fly tonight," Tāwera said.

"Me too. We must make sure it is fully dark before we sneak out."

"You do not seem so grumpy," Tāwera said, and it was obvious he'd chosen his words carefully.

"No. Thank you. I did not deserve your generosity."

Tāwera beamed. "Touching you in that way reminded me of better times when I assuaged the moonlust with Aroha and later flew with my mother."

Nyree pushed aside the instant turmoil that occurred as she imagined Tāwera with another woman. *Slippery slope.* "You must miss them. Manu should've replied to my email by now. I'll check after we eat. I'd better get those vegetables before Keith delivers them in person, and you need to hide."

There, that was better. She hadn't offered a hint of the jealous shrew.

Once Nyree returned, her inner chaos almost had her grabbing Tāwera for a repeat of earlier. It was his delicious scent. It did things to her. "I need a shower," she muttered and strode to the bathroom without looking back.

The moonlust... For the first time since the sex with Tāwera had happened, Nyree allowed herself to pull up memories. Awe-inspiring and so unlike her interactions with Ari. The bedroom problems she and Ari had suffered hadn't been her fault.

She wasn't a terrible lover.

At least, Tāwera hadn't complained.

And she had to stop thinking about sex with Ari or with Tāwera. She yanked at the shower tap and jumped under the stream of water before it warmed. Four minutes later, she was out and drying herself. She dressed rapidly and walked out to join Tāwera, her armor firmly in place.

When she powered up her tablet, Tāwera turned to her with eagerness.

"Can I push the buttons to make the letters come through?"

"Emails," she said as she shunted the tablet across the table.

His forehead scrunched into concentration lines as he tapped in her password and the correct apps to pull through her email. He looked so cute, despite the tattoos that made most people take two steps backward to avoid contact with him. He was a good man, a kind one, yet a fierce warrior lurked beneath his skin.

"You have new letters," he said. "Emails."

"Who are they from?" At first, he'd stumbled over words, but he was a fast learner.

"You have one from Manu, your cousin."

"Do you remember how to open the email?"

"Yes." Eagerness flashed in him, making her want to laugh.

"Open it for me and read it aloud while I start dinner preparations."

He frowned. "Is it not private?"

"I wrote to Manu for answers. They are to help both of us."

Tāwera nodded. "Dear Nyree," he began. "The contents of your email came as a tremendous surprise. I confided with Hone and his father, and they started an investigation. Your new friend came from a part of the world where the local missionaries kept excellent records, which has helped us considerably. Tāwera's sudden disappearance caused consternation amongst his tribe and the local missionaries, and one minister wrote about him in his diary. He disappeared on the eve of his wedding to a woman called Aroha, and the last person to see him was his half-brother, Rāwiri."

Tāwera paused, his low growl filling the lounge. "Because he tricked me and trapped me inside the rock."

"I know." Nyree patted his shoulder. "At least you're out now that we've broken the curse, and you can start living. What else does he say?"

"Rāwiri told everyone he'd completed the tattoo for Tāwera, and they'd parted. Tāwera had gone to meet with friends while Rāwiri said he'd strolled to the waterfront to see the new sailing ship that had arrived in port." Tāwera lifted his head to glance at her, anger digging into his features and hardening his jaw. "He spoke the truth. He walked to the port, but he took me with him and sold me to a sailor who worked on that ship."

"What else does Manu say?"

"The locals continued their search for several months. Tāwera's disappearance was a mystery that shocked everyone because of his popularity. Eventually, Rāwiri married Aroha, and they had three sons."

Tāwera released a grunt. "Your friend says he hasn't had time to trace the family tree. Rāwiri died in a drowning accident when a *waka* overturned. Aroha lived with her youngest son and his wife until her death at ninety-two."

"She married your brother. That's terrible," Nyree said. "Even though hundreds of years have passed, it must seem like yesterday to you."

"I still can't believe Rāwiri did this," Tāwera muttered.

"He was jealous of you and coveted what you had."

"Rāwiri asked Aroha's father if he could court her but later assured me he was fine when he learned Aroha and I were close and had been for some time."

"He lied."

"Yes," Tāwera agreed. "Your friend says you must take a photo of me if possible and send it to him. What is a passport?"

"It is a travel document. We can do that after dinner."

Tāwera nodded. "Manu says that once he has organized a passport, he will arrange airfares for me." He raised his gaze to stare at her. "He offers me a place to live while I become used to the modern world and any support I require. I am a stranger to him."

"My cousin, Manu, is an excellent leader." Nyree chopped a carrot, her knife slicing through the vegetable with a distinct crunch. "His family has helped our tribe become strong, and we support each other. He provides financial assistance for those who require it, helps with housing, jobs, and gives emotional aid when any of us have the need. He is a better leader than his mother."

"A woman led your tribe?"

"Yes, Manu had to kill her when she tried to murder his cousin's mate. I only know the basic details of what happened that night, but it took Manu a long time to move past the traumatic events. His father blamed him, but his brothers stood by Manu. His friends. Under Manu's direction, our tribe has become prosperous and started new initiatives to help the youngsters."

"Where were they when you needed help?"

"I'm beginning to understand I should've approached Manu earlier and asked for help when Ari became difficult. My pride got in the way. I thought I'd handle the situation, but everything escalated and became worse."

"Will we fly after dinner?"

"Yes, we'll go as soon as it is dark."

"I shall look forward to flying with you."

A dart of awareness pierced her then, and she wondered if she was imagining things or if Tāwera had meant more than what he'd said. Shaking her head, she continued dinner preparations. Tāwera was right about one thing. The sexual release had left her more grounded and more herself. Definitely in a better frame of mind. Unfortunately, it had also left an acute yearning to repeat the experience, which wouldn't do at all.

Tāwera continued reading Manu's email. Manu asked if he wanted to learn of his brother's children and what had happened to them. The knowledge that Rāwiri had married Aroha and they'd had children together bothered him. It was as if Rāwiri had stepped into his shoes and stolen Tāwera's life. He'd like to learn of his mother's fate if that was possible. Nyree had explained she'd leave here at the end of summer and return to New Zealand. He must be ready to go with her, and that presented problems now that he was conspicuous.

While he enjoyed learning new things and mastering the

machines Nyree used, he found the rapid pace disconcerting. The sheer number of things he had to learn scared him, although he hadn't confessed this to Nyree. He hated her to worry, but perhaps he could ask her friend.

The thing that bothered him the most was what would he do when he finally reached Aotearoa? The world he'd known no longer existed, and the busy place where he'd lived was now a sleepy town called Russell. It was full of people called tourists. He'd been a skilled fighter and hunter, but Nyree said most people lived in towns and cities. Fighting skills were no longer required in their homeland. If people disagreed about land, they settled the dispute in court. They negotiated a settlement.

How did he support himself? Where would he live, and how would he occupy his time?

And the most burning question of all—how could he walk away from Nyree?

Even before he'd helped her with her moonlust, he'd ached to touch her, to kiss her. He frowned. The strength of his need bothered him, given it was even greater than his memories of desiring Aroha. He'd been younger, and they hadn't been able to keep their hands off each other. With Nyree, the urges were stronger. Fiercer, and he struggled with restraint.

Tāwera mentioned none of this to Nyree because he hadn't wanted to worry her when he'd already caused a massive disruption in her life. Her agreeing to his touch had been a tremendous relief.

He'd been hanging onto his control with difficulty.

With this in mind, he turned to the only source he had. He slowly and painstakingly composed his own email and sent it back to Manu. He'd confess everything to Nyree after Manu sent him a reply, but he'd feel better to have advice from the tribal leader.

CHAPTER 12

That's a Lie

Nyree's mind and gaze kept slipping to Tāwera as he read his book. Sex with him had been different. Better and more fulfilling. It hadn't been merely the assuaging of her moonlust, but something powerful and enduring.

Stop it, Nyree. You're simply grateful for Tāwera's help. It's a crush, and you know better.

It was true. Ari had put her off anything resembling a relationship. It was too soon to think of another man. A crush. Just a stupid crush. Soon, Tāwera would go his own way. He'd make friends and start a job. They hadn't spoken of what he wanted to do once he reached home.

Nyree frowned. Her mother hadn't emailed recently, and Manu hadn't mentioned her mother or sister in the part of the email Tāwera had read to her. Later tonight, she'd make a point of emailing them again.

She made macaroni and cheese, added fresh vegetables for interest, and popped it into the oven before grabbing her tablet. She discovered a second email from Manu but read the first one's contents before opening the second.

"Ah," she muttered. Her mother and sister had gone to Taupo to spend two weeks with Nyree's auntie. Her auntie didn't have internet, a fact her cousins had bemoaned whenever Nyree saw them. She would've thought her sister would've sent her an email, though. She continued reading the results of Manu's research. He'd offered to have Tāwera stay with him and his wife until he got on his feet. Manu mentioned he and Jessalyn were eager to learn the older traditions that the tribes had lost.

Nyree closed that email and opened the second. Her eyes widened since Manu had addressed the email to Tāwera. Briefly, she struggled with the ethics of reading his email until she noticed Manu had mentioned her.

Mates?

A gasp escaped, and she slapped her hand over her mouth. She checked to assure herself Tāwera's book still claimed his focus. Even though she'd wondered, given their ability to communicate in taniwha form, she'd told herself she was imagining the possibility. A head in the sand reaction, for sure. Frowning, she continued reading.

Manu thought she and Tāwera were mates since Tāwera's reaction was similar to Manu's response when he'd encountered Jessalyn. He told Tāwera to speak with her because any attempt to resist their connection would worsen the moonlust. Her cousin added nature was seldom wrong when the bonds formed. He and Nyree were compatible and would have a good life together.

Mates?

Flabbergasted, she stared at the words. Manu was wrong.

She wasn't interested in jumping into a serious relationship with anyone, not after her Ari debacle.

Tāwera hadn't mentioned mates to her. Emma and Cassie had spoken to her about becoming mates with Jack and Hone. They'd all fought in their way, not wanting forever with one person. They'd had various reasons, but bottom line, not one of them had escaped fate.

She pressed her lips together to halt a scream. As much as she liked Tāwera and enjoyed his company, she didn't want forever. She wanted to travel, to do the things she'd always dreamed of, but Ari had refused to let her indulge her desires.

Anger pumped through her then. Fury at Ari for letting him box her into an emotional trap. For the *nth* time since leaving New Zealand, she chastised herself for buckling to Ari. Once she'd acted the obedient woman and he'd discovered her soft spots—her family—she'd been on unsteady ground because she'd wanted to protect her mother and sister.

And now, apparently, she had a mate.

Manu could be wrong.

Nyree thought about when they'd made love this afternoon—no, it had been plain sex. The physical contact had soothed every part of her angst and left her with increased strength. Happy.

She'd hoped to repeat the experience, but she'd thought of suggesting friends with benefits. A relationship to last only as long as her summer job. They might have remained friends, but now—it was impossible. She'd made a pact with herself never to rely on another man again. *Gah!* It was apparent she had faulty genes.

As much as she loved her mother and had promised herself never to follow in her parent's footsteps by trusting men who weren't worth the trouble, she'd found herself in that vulnerable place.

Never again.

Nyree stared at the email again and lifted her hand. Her finger hovered over the delete button. Then her mouth tightened to a determined line, and she deleted the email.

CHAPTER 13

Flight From Hell

Tāwera slid a puzzled glance at Nyree as she bustled around the kitchen. He wasn't sure what was wrong with her, but every one of his instincts screamed something was out of balance. Nyree was chatting with him. She was smiling, or at least her mouth curved upward. Her eyes were as cold as blocks of ice. She seemed...twitchy. That was the best description he could summon.

She set a meal in front of him. As usual, the food was foreign to him, but it smelled appetizing. "Thank you."

"You're welcome." Once again, her expression didn't match the words.

He opened his mouth to ask questions but pressed his lips

together as he decided to wait. Perhaps the moonlust affected her differently. He would observe. Maybe his email to Manu would yield results.

"Are you looking forward to flying tonight?" he asked.

"Yes."

A simple reply and nothing more. Tāwera stared down at his meal, no longer hungry. He ate anyway but didn't pepper Nyree with his questions.

Once they'd eaten, Nyree took his photo several times and emailed them to Manu. They did the dishes and cleaned the kitchen, then both read books to kill time.

The wait for complete darkness seemed endless, but he appreciated the necessity of secrecy. The more he learned of the world from the tablet, his reading, and his conversations with Nyree, the more he understood the need for stealth. This advanced world held things good and evil, the differences from what he'd known then to now vast. Questions pounded him, but he remained silent. No, it was best if he waited for Nyree to work out whatever bothered her. With Aroha, this approach had always worked best.

He thought back to the giggling girl he'd intended to marry and wondered how she'd fared with his brother. Had she been happy? Would marriage to Rāwiri have satisfied her? Had she cried when Tāwera had disappeared? So many queries for which he'd never know the answer.

Had Rāwiri wanted Aroha all along? Why hadn't he told Tāwera this at the start instead of lying? Tāwera had offered to carry Aroha's basket one day. Their relationship had started innocently, and they'd grown together in friendship, but if Rāwiri had told Tāwera of his interest, he would've stood back and let his brother court Aroha.

Looking back now, he thought his feelings for Aroha were that of lust and friendship. If they'd married, he would've done his best to make her happy. Now, learning the truth of what Rāwiri had done, he directed his anger at his brother. He hoped the marriage had contented Aroha, and she'd enjoyed her children, her grandchildren.

"What's wrong?" Nyree asked. "You've been staring at the same page for the last five minutes."

"I was wondering about my brother and Aroha. I hope Aroha's life pleased her."

"And your brother?"

"I wish he'd given me the truth instead of plotting behind my back. We were different, had diverse strengths, and neither of us was better than the other. I never thought of Rāwiri as my competitor. He was my brother."

"He thought differently."

"I knew he had a cunning side, and he manipulated people, but I never suspected he'd betray me this way."

"But you ended up imprisoned inside the rock. You told me your brother did this."

Tāwera contorted his face hard enough to feel the grimace. "A tiny part of me has always hoped the curse was a mistake or an error of judgment."

"Don't you think the fact that Rāwiri sold you to a sailor pointed the finger directly at nefarious reasons?"

"True, but I'd hoped Rāwiri had an explanation."

Nyree's brows arched toward her hairline. "Like what? He tattooed a curse on your back by mistake?"

"He told me one of his friends had helped him with the intricate design."

Nyree snorted this time. "Your brother played a part in the curse. Admit it. Chances are it was his idea, his plan, although you'll never know what he was thinking."

"That's the part that frustrates me," Tāwera confessed. "This anger pulses in me, and I have nowhere to direct my wrath. It's most unsatisfactory."

"Yes, it must be," Nyree said and set her book aside. "It's dark enough for us to fly now. It's probably best for us to walk a distance from here before we shift and take off."

"You know best," Tāwera said. "I hope my transformation is easier this time. Is there any food we can take with us and leave with our clothes, ready for our return? Eating seems to help."

"Sure, I'll grab something now. Do you want to wait for me outside? Your hearing is better than mine. I've noticed the new group of scientists wander at all hours. One of them is studying the stars or clouds. I couldn't quite understand the technical terms he used."

Tāwera barked out a laugh. He'd spotted the men loitering, trying to grab Nyree's attention. She'd treated them with friendliness and politeness and nothing more, showing no preference for one over another. Her aloofness had challenged them, so it was no wonder they were everywhere, trying to grab her attention. "I shall wait for you outside."

He stepped outdoors and listened carefully. He heard the single bark of a seal and a high-pitched reply from a pup. The wind whistled over the top of the hills surrounding Grytviken, creating a mournful whistle. A lonely sound. As usual, the area was ripe with animal smells. Tāwera heard or scented nothing else to alarm him.

"Can we go?" Nyree murmured when she joined him. She, too, wore dark clothes to blend with the night. She'd even changed her typical day pack for a black cloth carry bag.

"I can't hear anyone. Which direction will we go?"

"Let's walk toward the graveyard. That way, if anyone spots one of us and asks questions, we can say we wanted to search for Shackleton's ghost."

"You should not mock," Tāwera said. "Our legends tell of spirits who march to the tip of New Zealand and slip into the sea to journey to the home of our ancestors. For all we know, the ghosts of Antarctica explorers travel here."

Nyree's smile faded. "You are right, but it is still wise to go in that direction. If we walk to the church, we must pass the scientist's living quarters. One of them mentioned I do a lot of walking and we should go together next time."

Tāwera didn't comment, but a fit of uncharacteristic jealousy swept him, and he clenched his teeth so hard, his jaw ached.

Unwarranted wrath, too, since Nyree never flirted with the men of knowledge.

She was friendly and nothing more, which was why he shoved aside his resentment. Now that he was visible, his life had become way more complicated, and he disliked the necessity to sneak everywhere.

Hopefully, Manu would get him this passport thing soon. Nyree had explained he was an unauthorized visitor, and she wasn't sure of the protocol. The United Kingdom ruled South Georgia and their laws applied here, even though they didn't have lawmen onsite. Nyree had told him she'd do some research on this area and read the manual on rules and regulations.

After pausing to listen for anything out of the ordinary, they slipped through the darkness. Their taniwha heritage gave them excellent eyesight, and they avoided sleeping seals and drowsy penguins. A few birds woke and shuffled out of their way but soon settled once they realized he and Nyree meant no harm.

Tāwera followed Nyree over the grass and the winding stream.

They kept walking once they reached the cemetery and followed the white fence, Nyree leading him up the craggy slope beyond the graveyard.

"I went for a walk this way three days ago. Keith told me the view from this hill is into the next bay. Hopefully, that will work for our purposes. It's best not to fly from the same spot all the time."

"I agree," Tāwera said.

The climb became more of a scramble, but they clambered over the rocks and higher to the peak. The tiny bay beyond was not appropriate for a boat landing, but it suited their purposes.

"Let's leave our clothes here," Nyree said. "They should be safe enough in this crevice and stay dry and undisturbed."

"As long as nothing eats the food," Tāwera said as he removed his clothes and footwear. He folded his T-shirt and trousers and handed them to Nyree. She gathered her clothes and placed them all in her bag.

"Ready?" she asked, standing back after securing their possessions inside the crevice.

Tāwera inhaled and released his breath on a loud sigh. "Ready, but I don't have the same exhilaration I normally associate with a full moon flight."

"Maybe it's the weather," Nyree said.

"I've never had this peculiar sense before."

"Perhaps it's because this is your first full moon since we broke the curse."

Tāwera shrugged and stood back to give himself room. He hoped the more he shifted, the easier it would become.

He'd been so wrong.

This shift troubled him worse than the previous one, and he had to force back his panic and regather his thoughts. It was only Nyree who pulled him from utter terror and chaos. She moved into the narrow tunnel of his vision. Her dragon lips moved as if she were speaking to him, but he didn't comprehend.

Yet he heard her emotions—if that were possible—and sensed the urgency emanating from her.

Her will prevailed.

The last half of his shift proceeded with such force, it left him panting and weak.

"Are you well?" Nyree's concern slipped into his mind, once again helping him to center and push away the worst of the pain.

He forced himself to take slow and even breaths until his nerve endings ceased their violent complaints and merely quivered. It took long moments before he dared to move a muscle.

"Tāwera, can you fly? Should we return home?"

Nyree thinking of him instead of others. *"No, you need to fly. It will help you stabilize and decrease the effect of the moonlust."*

"But what about you?"

"I'll wait here until I can move. I must fly too, even if it's painful."

"Has this happened before?"

"Never. I've never had problems with shifting or flying before,

never suffered this agony. My gut says if I try to avoid flying and shifting, the symptoms will become worse."

"This is not a common phenomenon," Nyree said.

"Have you ever heard of a warrior encased in a stone curse? No, me neither," he muttered.

Nyree nuzzled his neck, taking care to graze his black scales with gentle pressure instead of causing him further pain. "I get your point."

"Fly. Enjoy the full moon. You need to steady your dragon. Let me worry about myself."

"No, I—"

"Please, Nyree. Just do as I ask."

Nyree brushed her nose against his in the taniwha form of a hongi.

Then, she backed up and propelled herself upward, her black wings flapping slowly and gradually increasing in speed. She lifted with a sexy twitch of her tail, and Tāwera's heart went with her. This woman slayed him with her beauty, her generosity, her selfless help to a confused Māori warrior.

Tāwera stretched his neck and moaned softly at the arc of pain that darted toward his tail. He swallowed hard, every one of his instincts telling him to curl into a ball and give in to the torment. He fought with his mind while scarcely daring to breathe.

Was it the curse again? Was he going to lose everything? Lose Nyree when he'd just found her?

No.

He refused to let that happen. Tāwera forced himself to move in small increments. He gritted his teeth and attempted to center his mind as he used to do when he was shifting. The agony didn't lessen, but it didn't become worse either. He continued to pull up a screen, brick by brick, until the wall surrounded him. The instant he completed the barrier, the pain deadened, and he took a deep, sustaining breath.

Next, Tāwera focused on pushing out the walls and giving himself more space.

He needed to fly and join Nyree as she soared through the sky. A sliver of determination jumped into the gap where the discomfort had been.

Tāwera expanded his lungs, focused his mind once again, and leaped into the air. He ignored the flash of soreness as he beat his wings. The pain continued, jabbing at his confidence and pushing him to return to land. No stopping because he suspected after a halt, he'd have difficulty trying again.

"Tāwera, move your wings faster," Nyree instructed. *"Push yourself harder, or else your body won't lift."*

Tāwera focused on her sweet voice and attempted to follow her instructions. *It hadn't been this difficult last time.* He increased the speed of his wings and almost cried out when his bulky body rose. Every flap of his wings brought a wince, but at least he was flying, and he was with Nyree. He focused on her scent and the friendship they'd forged since they'd met. He recalled the conversations they'd had, and most of all, he remembered the way she'd fit in his arms. The way her mouth moved against his and how much he wanted to hold and touch her again.

His body rose, and with this came relief.

Nyree, his lodestone.

His everything.

The more effort he put into flying, the easier he pushed back against the torture in his bones and muscles. He soared toward Nyree, his heart still full of that determination and now joy because he was beating this sudden handicap of his.

With Nyree at his side, he could do anything. He firmly believed this, which meant he must fight for her, fight this stupid curse and walk with confidence into the future.

"You're doing great," Nyree said. *"Is the pain gone?"*

"No, it's still there, but it's more manageable." Thanks to Nyree.

"Are you ready to fly farther?"

"Yes," he said, confidence shading his words when he wasn't sure he had the strength to swat a gnat.

"Fly at my side. I want to make sure you're okay before I soar at will."

"Go. I will fly for a bit longer and wait for you by our clothes." It might take him a while to shift again—he needed to find his nerve after this disaster.

"Are you certain?" Once again, concern filled her words.

"Go ahead." He forced out the words when he wanted to demand she stay with him. It was what Rāwiri would've done, and immediately, Tāwera fought the impulse. Without warning, he dropped. A startled roar escaped him. Flames shot from his open maw even as he struggled to control his plummet.

"Tāwera!"

Nyree's voice forced through his panic, and he pulled out of the plunge seconds before he collided with a wall of rock.

"What were you thinking?" Her shout slapped some sense into him, and he directed his body away from the rock face.

Tāwera shook his massive head, shocked by his near-miss. His thoughts scrambled as he admitted he wasn't himself. *"I think I have flown enough. My energy has faded."*

"I'll come back now too," Nyree said. *"We can fly again tomorrow."*

Tāwera made a noncommittal sound through their mind-bond while he battled his worry. He'd thought he'd escaped the curse, but something was very wrong.

Tāwera thought back. He'd felt fine earlier in the day—this afternoon. Yes, it was only this evening when sluggishness had crept upon him. At first, he hadn't noticed or recognized the signs. It was when he'd shifted the full effects had struck him over the head.

Instead of worrying, he focused on each wing beat. Not much farther to go now. To his left, he spotted three lights glowing from the settlement. The rest of the island lay in blackness, the wind and the sea creating the only sounds. The waves whooshed to shore, curling and crashing against rocks. One more wing beat. Another.

Exhaustion turned his limbs and body to onerous weights, and he struggled to continue.

"Tāwera, keep going. We're almost there. Another five minutes at most."

Apprehension carried in her voice, spiking his own anxiety because he didn't think he'd make it. They skimmed the landscape, barely clearing the peaks.

"Keep flying," Nyree said, her voice calmer this time. "I can see the spot where we took off."

Tāwera strained to exert force with his wings. He remained in flight but barely cleared the craggy rocks littering the landscape. He couldn't avoid the next pile of stones, and he grunted as they gouged his stomach. For an instant, his wings ceased flapping.

He struck the ground and landed in a heap, too stunned to feel anything except shock.

"Tāwera, are you okay?" Nyree landed beside him and shifted. "Turn over. No, even better, try to shift."

"Can't."

"You haven't even tried," she snapped. "Shift right now." She pinched the tender skin under his belly hard enough to make him groan. "Move now."

He tried to push past the pain, but the fiery agony robbed him of his focus.

"Tāwera! I will not lose you. You will not die while I'm here. I saved you from the curse, and you have to get past this. You have an entire life to live. You have an opportunity—a second chance—and if you do nothing, you're throwing it away." She kicked him in the ribs as if to emphasize her point.

He grunted. *"That hurt."*

"Then you know you're still alive."

Excellent point, and she was right. He couldn't lie here like a rock. Nyree had to return and rest before work the next day.

When the pain evened out to a tolerable level, he visualized his two-legged form and locked onto the image. This time pressure pushed at him, and he almost lost his focus. *A bit longer. Hold it for a little longer. Once you return to your human form, you'll be okay. Nyree can help you get back to her place.*

Nyree placed her hand on his back, and her touch centered him. The pain receded enough for him to concentrate on his shift. Suddenly, he was more human than taniwha, the more troublesome part of the change done. He continued to pour his will into the transformation, and his form condensed, morphing into his human body.

"Great job," Nyree said. "Here are your clothes. You'd better dress fast before you shiver again."

His hands shook so badly that Nyree helped him to stand. Once again, her proximity aided him to stabilize, and when her palm cupped his shoulder, his throbbing faded.

This time, his groan was one of pleasure. "Your touch makes the torment vanish."

She cocked her head. "Are you certain it's not the shift giving you relief?"

"Stand back. I can manage my clothes on my own." He stepped into his trousers before she released her grip on his shoulder.

Nyree backed up, and the explosion of pain took him out at the knees.

She frowned as she rushed to his side. "You know what this reminds me of?"

"No." Tāwera panted out the reply.

"I once saw a woman with an extreme case of moonlust. She refused to masturbate for relief, and because of her religious convictions, she would not have sex before marriage. Flying wasn't possible for her, and she suffered in the same way as you."

"But I flew," Tāwera said. "It was painful, so much so that it was difficult to remember to move my wings. Shifting should counteract the moonlust."

Nyree grasped his arm, and the warmth emanating from her body eased most of the agony. She helped him pull his T-shirt into position and continued with the physical contact while he laced up his shoes. "Perhaps the curse has interrupted how moonlust affects you?"

Tāwera scowled. "You think Rāwiri's curse is clinging to me?"

"It's a theory. Come on. Let's go home." She clasped hands with him. "I'm starving. We can eat an energy bar while we walk."

They scrambled down the hill, retaining physical contact the entire way. Once they reached flat ground, Nyree pulled the energy bars from her pocket and handed one to Tāwera.

"I'm going to release your hand. Maybe you haven't eaten enough."

Tāwera didn't think this was the case. He opened his mouth to refute her suggestion and thought better of it. Nyree was right. They should try every variation and rule out each possibility one by one. He accepted the bar she handed him and bit down. It was chewy and full of fruit. Sweetness burst across his tongue.

"The food is much sweeter than I am used to," he said.

"Sugar is a problem in the modern world. On average, people are taller and bigger than our ancestors. You fit in with your height and breadth."

"I was larger than most of the warriors, but I thought my taniwha heritage was responsible for my size."

"A possibility," Nyree agreed. "Has eating helped?"

"I'm about the same." He released her hand and walked at her side rather than touching her.

The pain level shot upward, and he grimaced. It wasn't as sharp as before, but gradually, it would overwhelm him again. He groped for her hand, the relief instantaneous.

"Interesting," Nyree said.

Yes, it was fascinating, and he could think of one more thing they hadn't tried this evening. He turned to her and spotted the knowledge in her expressive eyes.

"Sex," he said.

CHAPTER 14

Let's Take a Shower

Tāwera's grip tightened on hers, and in an unspoken agreement, they increased their pace, picking their way through the moonlit rocky landscape toward the cemetery. Her heart beat faster, and arousal slid through her veins with every inhalation of the salty tang of sea air. A hint of taniwha and Tāwera's green scent reached her, driving her desire to fever pitch. Despite knowing this was a bad idea, she intended to sleep with him tonight. She could tell herself this was an experiment to learn if sex helped to steady Tāwera, but the truth was she ached for him.

Once was not enough, not when it had been so fast.

No, Nyree craved a night together where they learned what each liked best. A night where she could touch at will and explore his magnificent body without restrictions. She craved his caresses in return. A slow loving. A tender one, plus a little fast and furious action to warm them up.

"Are you sure you want to do this?" Tāwera broke into her musing over which type of loving she'd prefer first.

"It is for my benefit too. I like you, and if we can help each other this way, I have no objections to physical contact between us."

"Thank you."

Nyree nudged him with her hip as they walked along the sandy and rock-strewn beach. Gentle waves whooshed to shore, threatening to dampen their boots. "Thanks are unnecessary. In my time, we call this friends with benefits. It is a mutual agreement to sleep with each other until one of us wishes to call off the relationship. It is sex without complications."

"I see."

Nyree shot Tāwera a sideward glance and caught his frown. "Sex and relationships are different in our time. No one will censor us if we sleep together without the commitment of marriage."

"This is common?"

"Yes, a lot of couples live together, but for various reasons, never get married. They have children and are like a regular family, but they do it without the benefit of a marriage."

"Your time is strange," Tāwera said as they approached the settlement.

By common consent, they slowed and listened for any of the scientists. Not one wandered outside to study the stars or the penguins or anything else. All was quiet as they crept past Keith and Carolyn's prefab building. A distinct snore sounded, followed by a masculine grumble. Nyree giggled and slapped her free hand over her mouth.

Tāwera dragged her through the shadows, his steps more certain now. Confident. A combo of the food and physical touch, or maybe it was the promise of the intimacy to come. Nyree wasn't sure, but the same eagerness had her striding at his side.

Their steps slowed as they approached her place, and they listened for foreign sounds. Tāwera nodded, and Nyree opened her door. They stepped inside before turning on a light and removing their footwear.

Nyree laughed when she saw Tāwera more clearly. "You look terrible. Come, we'll have a shower. You'll be sore tomorrow. It looks as if you bled through your shirt. Let me have a look."

The wound wasn't as bad as she'd expected, but it bled sluggishly.

"I used to heal faster," Tāwera said.

"All right, but we can't count on you having the same benefits from your taniwha heritage now. It pains you to shift. That is not normal."

"I want sex," Tāwera said bluntly.

When she glanced at him again, she spotted the tenting of

his trousers. "Shower first," she said. "I'm sweaty and want to shower." She took his hand and led him to the bathroom. She'd give him part of what he needed now and indulge herself in exploring his body at the same time.

In the plain bathroom, she tugged off his T-shirt and unfastened the fly of his trousers. She maneuvered the fabric over his erection, and he let her. Once he was naked, she shunted him toward the shower. "Wash off the blood while I undress."

He turned on the shower and followed her instructions without argument. Nyree took a moment to enjoy the vision. He was all sleek muscles and masculinity, and not even his bumps and scrapes spoiled the spectacular sight. She hustled out of her clothes and opened the door to join him in the cubicle. She washed briskly before turning her attention to Tāwera again. The scrapes on his belly had healed a fraction. The skin had knitted together enough for her to cease worrying about first-aid.

Reassured, she gave into temptation and ran her hands over his shoulders and down his arms. When she cupped his hips, her gaze slipped to his erection. Broad and rigid and almost beautiful, the head swollen and perfect for what she ached to do next. Using his body for balance, she kneeled in front of him. Her fingers traced the lines and whorls of tattoos on his buttocks. The tattoos, created in the old way with toothed combs and mallets, had fashioned a tapestry of decorative scars with intense personal meaning. She couldn't wait to explore them with her tongue. Tāwera watched her the entire time, his brown eyes full of questions.

She didn't give him time to voice them but took his cock into her mouth. He groaned, the masculine sound reverberating in the cubicle.

She smiled up at him as much as she could with her mouth full of masculine flesh. His eyes were wide now, and she got the sense this was something new to him. Nyree gripped his thickly muscled thighs and set about teasing him. She licked and sucked and glanced up when his hands came down to tangle in her hair.

"I didn't know this would feel so good," he whispered.

Another experience for him. Satisfaction writhed through her as she upped the pace. Her breasts grew swollen and heavy, and she ached for more, but first, she wanted Tāwera to have this pleasure. Ari had liked her sucking him off, but he'd been rough and enjoyed pushing her until she'd almost choked. Tāwera held himself still, and she pulled off his shaft to glance up at him.

"You can move but let me control how deep you thrust. Okay?"

Still wide-eyed, he nodded, and she resumed her teasing. She licked and stroked, taking him deep and using her tongue to torment him. His bulky thighs started to tremble, and his hips jerked in involuntary thrusts. He groaned and shuddered, and she continued her torture by stroking him and pressing firmly on a spot she knew would push him higher.

"Nyree," he gasped. "I'm going to explode."

Excellent. Seconds later, he came with a gasp. Nyree swallowed and continued to stroke until he stilled.

"Nyree," he whispered again, his hands cradling and caressing her head now.

She released him and rose. His arms came around her, and they kissed.

The water had gone cold, but she didn't care. They were clean now, and that was all that mattered. She turned off the water and reached for a towel. She dried Tāwera, taking particular care around his scrapes.

They no longer bled, although he wasn't healing as rapidly as she did from injuries. Nyree dried herself and took Tāwera's hand to lead him to the bedroom.

"How are your ouchies?"

He grimaced. "I need more."

"More sex?"

"My body is still throbbing. It is strange. The level of pain eased after you took me in your mouth, but I'm still off-balance, and I need more to regain my normal level."

"Let's have more then," Nyree said.

They toppled onto the mattress together, and Tāwera took her into his arms. Their mouths met, and Nyree fell into their kiss. It was soft and tender, bold and seductive. It was everything she'd ever wanted from a kiss, and she clung to him. He ran his hands down her back, and she felt safe and happy. She felt loved.

Nyree paused as that thought rushed through her mind.

Tāwera didn't love her. She didn't want his love or anyone's love.

Friendship—yes. But love wasn't for her. She wanted her independence, and after Ari's example, she figured she was best on her own.

Tāwera's hands wandered everywhere, stroking her back, her arse, and her thighs. Heat built in her as they continued to kiss. She'd thought Tāwera would hurry since he'd mentioned his eagerness. But he didn't push for speed. He seemed content to build their passion layer upon layer before it overwhelmed them both. Nyree shuddered and gasped, dug her fingernails into Tāwera's back.

He grunted in return and hastened the pace of his strokes. With each thrust, he hit the right spot, and Nyree couldn't hold on any longer.

She plunged into her orgasm, the pleasure/pain so sharp, she froze.

Tāwera thrust twice more and stilled too, his big body shaking. He held her tight—too tight—but his possessive touch was exactly what she needed right now. The comfort and intimacy that came with sexual release had always eluded her with Ari. It was different with Tāwera because she could be herself instead of worrying if she'd set off his temper.

He kissed her shoulder and separated their bodies before tugging her back against his chest.

"Do you ever lose your temper?" she asked.

"Most people do at some stage," he replied, his finger tracing patterns over her upper arm. "Whenever I think of what Rāwiri did, my anger rises."

"Not surprising," she said lightly. "How are you now?"

"The pain has vanished," Tāwera said. "It faded as soon as we started kissing and touching."

"That's weird. Do you think the sexual high helped, or is this just a coincidence? I wonder if you can shift without discomfort now? Perhaps the curse *has* disrupted your taniwha, and your needs have changed. You said your brother didn't know of your dragon heritage. He wouldn't have factored this into his curse. This might be the reason you've come to life now." She pulled a face. "I guess you'll never understand what he did or the effects of the curse. You must go with the flow, as we say here."

"In the past, flying or sex helped to control my taniwha. My shifts were the same as yours. I'll experiment tomorrow while you're working. I worried that I'd fade again, but my body is remaining solid and visible."

"All the better for me. It's more satisfying making love to you now that I can see you properly."

Tāwera kissed her shoulder. "Sleep. You have work tomorrow, and it's past midnight."

"I'm glad you're here," Nyree whispered, her eyes refusing to stay open. She sank into sleep, happy and content. Secure in

Tāwera's arms.

Tāwera woke her in the morning, not long before her alarm was due to go off. He kissed her breasts and trailed his fingers through her dampness. They rocked together, gradually scaling the heights before dropping into freefall and pleasure. As their heartbeats slowed, Nyree lifted her head and offered her lips.

Their kiss sent another surge of pleasure swooping through her. She pulled back and stared into his eyes, studying his face for signs of pain.

"How are you this morning?"

"Better than I have been since you broke the curse," he said. "Cavorting with you is good for my health."

She laughed, then groaned when the alarm on her cell phone signaled it was time for her to hustle. She turned it off, dallied to kiss Tāwera again before she forced herself to slide out of bed. Nyree padded into the bathroom and stepped under the shower. It didn't surprise her when Tāwera joined her.

"Are you still going flying this morning?" she asked as she picked up the soap.

He took the soap from her and turned her to wash her back. "Yes, it's important for me to understand this new reaction to moonlust. If I wish to fit into this world, I must understand my physical needs. I am lucky I found you, or you found me rather than a man. I am beyond lucky that you like me enough to share your body with me."

"You're helping me too," she said, but she comprehended his meaning, and she wondered if she'd have been as generous with him if he wasn't an attractive man. Thankfully, she hadn't needed to face that dilemma.

After showering, they ate breakfast together before Nyree departed to start her morning of work. Tāwera left at the same time, and after grabbing a quick kiss, he slipped into the shadows, slowly making his way through the settlement and walking toward the church.

Carolyn was already at the museum and busy dusting when Nyree arrived to do a walk-through.

"Did I see you kissing a man a few minutes ago?" Carolyn asked, her tone both curious and full of humor.

Nyree froze. *Yikes. What should she say?*

Carolyn laughed. "I didn't get a good look at him. Which scientist is he? A few of them were showing interest in you."

"Um," Nyree said, stalling for time while she frantically tried to work out a reply.

"Ah, you're keeping things on the down-low."

"Yes," Nyree agreed. Luckily, Carolyn seemed content to tease Nyree.

"Probably a good idea. You don't want them fighting amongst each other or any stupid male posturing."

"No." No, she did not want that. She'd had enough trouble with Ari and his jealousy. She hated the thought of anyone fighting over her as if she was a piece of meat.

"You can bring him to dinner," Carolyn said. "Keith and I want to meet this mystery man. We've noticed you seem much happier than you were when we first arrived on the island. You've always been polite and a hard worker, but now you smile more readily, and it's lovely to see. I'm also impressed that you're continuing your excellent timekeeping and haven't let a romance impede your professionalism."

"Ah..."

"Look at the time." Carolyn tutted. "The ship is due in half an hour. How is the stock in the store?"

"I stocked up last night before I finished for the day," Nyree said. "Everything is ready."

"Excellent. We can whiz through the dusting together, and we'll have time to have a quick cup of tea with Keith. You can tell us about your man-friend. What sort of scientist did you say he was, dear?"

She had said nothing yet. "He's from New Zealand," Nyree said, redirecting the subject.

"Is he?" Carolyn beamed. "How nice."

In reply, Nyree grabbed a fluffy duster and retreated to the far end of the display. Somehow, she needed to think of a suitable story in the next ten minutes before facing Keith's and Carolyn's interrogation. No pressure or anything.

CHAPTER 15

The Past Attacks

Tāwera walked the familiar, dusty path toward the tiny white church at the hill's base, adeptly avoiding most scientists and other workers who frequented the settlement. It was the transient nature of the scientists that meant he could come and go at will. He'd encountered several of the men, and they'd stopped and chatted with him. He and Nyree had prepared for this, and his cover story that he was studying weather patterns seemed to work.

This morning, he lifted his hand in greeting and continued walking, Nyree's day pack draped over his shoulder. It contained water and a snack, plus it was a handy way of keeping his clothes dry because the weather down here shifted moods from sunny to

196

rainy without warning.

Once he reached the top of the hill and gazed over the settlement, he noted a sleek blue-and-white cruise ship slowing at the entrance of the bay to give way to a pod of humpback whales. He'd listened to Nyree's tales of the whalers and the pursuit of their prey in this bay. It was agreeable to see their return now and the increased population.

As he watched, one whale leaped from the water and made a tremendous splash. He grinned and watched a little longer before he continued to trek higher into the mountains. By the time he reached the mouth of a valley with ocean views, the whale pod had departed, and the cruise ship had disgorged its passengers.

Tāwera stripped and stuffed his clothes into the daypack. An instant later, he stood taller and centered his mind. This time, his shift was almost pain-free and seamless. With a mental whoop, he rose and flew inland over rocks covered in patches of melting snow. Interesting. It seemed as if Nyree was right, and the curse had adjusted his needs. Instead of shifting to his taniwha form, sex played into the equation.

He flew for an hour, soaring over snow-covered mountain peaks and exploring the island. Despite the milder weather, not much grew on the lower slopes.

A few mosses and lichen clung to rocks and provided a touch of color. Nyree had mentioned reindeer—four-legged animals—used to graze the slopes, but a team of hunters had killed them all to maintain the balance of nature. He hadn't known what a reindeer was until Nyree had shown him pictures and told him tales of Santa Claus. It reminded him of how much he still had to learn, although Nyree showed great patience with him.

Tāwera wondered what he might do when he returned to Aotearoa, but Nyree had instructed him not to worry. Manu and her other friends would help him to settle and make his way in the unfamiliar world, which reminded him. He must check Nyree's tablet to learn if Manu had written to him.

Aware of the passing time, he flew back to his clothes, shifted, and dressed. With the cruise passengers in port, he could wander at will, chat with them, and eavesdrop to increase his knowledge. He enjoyed these encounters and hearing the different accents and languages.

When he reached the path by the church, he passed several passengers. Most dressed in bright jackets. He'd wondered aloud why they wore identical clothing. Nyree had told him the cruise ships' owners issued their passengers with jackets and boots to ensure they had suitable waterproof gear.

He entered the church since he hadn't explored the interior yet. Two women stared at him, and he nodded in acknowledgment. His face, he realized. Too bad. He couldn't and didn't want to undo his *moko* since they were a badge of honor, and he'd worked hard to earn them.

"Excuse me," one woman said, drawing near enough for Tāwera

to get a whiff of her floral perfume.

He smiled politely and waited.

"Your tattoos are unusual. They're tribal, aren't they?" she asked, her expression alive with interest.

"Yes, they are part of my New Zealand heritage," he said.

"Can we take your photo?"

"No," Tāwera said. "I do not enjoy having my photo taken. It was nice to speak with you," he said, smiling to soften his rejection. He turned his back and wandered through the church. It was small but held the same hushed atmosphere of the one he'd known all those years ago.

Once Tāwera left, he wandered through the settlement, listening to the tourists' chatter as he headed to the store. He wasn't sure if Nyree would be working in there or if Carolyn would be on duty. He tried to keep his distance from Carolyn and Keith in case they asked nosy questions about him. To his delight, Nyree was selling stamps and postcards to a group of tourists.

She lifted her head when he entered and flashed a grin.

Mine, he thought with satisfaction.

He browsed the items, pretending to shop while listening to the tourists discussing their trip and gossiping with each other. When Nyree remained busy with a line of visitors waiting to purchase items, he drifted outside and toward the cemetery. He paused with another group of tourists to watch a group of king penguins as they decided if they'd jump into the water. The birds bunched together on a rock, packing tightly until the ones at the front of the group fell into the sea.

Tāwera laughed with the others until he felt the weight of a stare. Moving carefully, he repositioned himself so he could scan faces. He froze as he spotted a familiar figure in the crowd.

Rāwiri.

What? How?

Tāwera's stomach bucked, and emotions bombarded him as he gaped at the man. Shock. Fear. Anger. Confusion. Tāwera continued to stare. Rāwiri gave a polite nod and moved onward.

Not Rāwiri, he realized, but someone who resembled his half-brother so closely they had to be related. This man moved differently and didn't bear the same strutting confidence as his brother. Not the same *mana*. His clothes were modern, and when Tāwera scrutinized him more closely, he recognized subtle differences in features and physique.

Who was he?

Tāwera followed at a distance, his instincts twitching the longer he observed the man. He wasn't behaving like the other tourists. He didn't chat with the passengers, nor did he take photos with a camera or a phone. Instead, he scanned faces as if he were searching for someone. Tāwera trailed and spotted how the man tensed as he grew close enough to study the shop's interior.

Tāwera drew nearer and walked right past the stranger. He took the two steps leading into the store at a jog, and still, the man didn't look his way or tear his attention from whatever he found so interesting.

Tāwera entered and pretended to browse the postcards. They sat in a rack and put him at the right angle to watch the man.

Nyree finished serving her customer and glanced in Tāwera's direction with a smile. Tāwera shook his head and hoped she understood not to treat him as someone familiar.

"How much does it cost to post a letter to Aotearoa?" he asked.

She gawked at him for an instant before answering his question. Tāwera pointed to the rack of postcards so the man watching Nyree would assume he was a tourist asking questions.

"Nyree," Tāwera spoke in an undertone. "Can you describe Ari for me?

Nyree stilled, her face paling. "What?"

A customer approached the counter and placed two T-shirts, a polo shirt, and a notebook down before pulling out their wallet. "You finish with the gentleman," the woman said.

"It's all right," Tāwera said. "I need to write my postcard first. You go ahead." He backed up, taking a postcard with him, and angled his body to a position where he could watch the stranger.

He had vanished.

Instead of relief, tension rose in Tāwera. He didn't have a good feeling about this. It was something in the way the man had searched. His target might be another customer, but Tāwera didn't think so. He waited until there was a break in the customers before he approached Nyree.

"You think Ari is here?" Nyree's face remained devoid of color, and her gaze kept darting over Tāwera's shoulder to study the passersby.

"I thought it was my brother," Tāwera said. "That's what drew my attention."

Nyree forced a smile for a customer. She rang up the sale and accepted the correct cash in UK pounds before the customer left.

Three more chatting customers lined up for Nyree, and Tāwera drifted away to watch for the stranger. He couldn't see him, but his warrior senses pinged with awareness. The man was out there and watching, lurking in the shadows.

Tāwera shifted closer and waited to gain Nyree's attention. He signaled he was leaving. She'd remain safe while she was working. The ships usually stayed for around four to five hours before they left again. They'd wait until the ship left, and Nyree would be safe.

Ari was here?

Nyree's pulse raced, and her hands trembled as she gathered the two T-shirts and the notepad her current customer had placed on the counter. She offered a strained smile to the redhead who had a pert nose and a citrus scent wafting from her person. Nyree served her customer, but her mind was elsewhere.

No, it couldn't be Ari. How would he know where she'd gone?

The answer presented itself almost immediately.

Her mother.

Her parent was the weak link here. She'd believe Ari's silken tales of woe, and by the time he'd finished, her mother would agree Nyree was at fault for the breakup, that her daughter had made a serious mistake. Ari possessed charm and understood how to use it with women. It was why he never had a shortage of feminine attention. Unfortunately, it had taken her too long to appreciate his charisma was only skin-deep while the place where his heart should be was full of darkness.

But how could he be here?

No, it couldn't be Ari.

She dragged in a citrus-scented breath and forced herself to release it and repeat the process.

Perhaps Tāwera was wrong, and it was Rāwiri, his brother. Somehow, he'd traveled through time or extended his life. After all, this was no crazier than a curse or Tāwera's sudden appearance.

The cruise ship left around six this evening. All she needed to do was continue working and wait for everyone to leave. Whoever this stranger was, they had to depart with the ship.

Yes, she was stressing over nothing.

She and Ari were done, and once he got over his pride, he'd understand this was for the best. He'd have no trouble finding a replacement—if he hadn't already. She'd ask Manu to check.

Between customers, she managed a quick email to Manu. To her relief, her message went through straightaway. Now all she had to do was wait for a reply, confirmation Ari was still at home in Papakura and that he was harassing another woman now.

She wished her mother or her sister were better correspondents so she'd know they were okay. It helped tremendously to know Manu and Jessalyn were nearby and watching over them. If it weren't for that fact, her panic levels would be much higher.

Carolyn entered the store and waited until she finished serving a customer. "Take a fifteen-minute break. I'll look after things here for you."

"What about the tour?"

Carolyn grinned. "It starts in half an hour, so don't be late back from your break."

"Thanks," Nyree said. "I'll be at my place if you need me."

"No problem. See you in fifteen." Carolyn shunted her out of the way and took over serving the line of customers.

Nyree paused on the deck outside the store and surveyed her surroundings. She didn't see anyone or thing out of place. Neither could she see Tāwera, so she rushed down the stairs and jogged to her home. She unlocked the door and locked it again once she darted inside.

Her stomach rumbled, but she ignored her body's signal to peek through the windows and scan the crowds of passengers exploring the area. When she found nothing out of place or suspicious, she retraced her footsteps to the kitchen and opened her fridge. Food. She pulled out the remains of a meaty stew and heated it in the microwave.

A tap at the door had her stiffening, and a gasp escaped before she could stop it. Her pulse raced, and she hesitated.

"Nyree, it's me. Tāwera," came the low masculine voice.

Nyree rushed to the door and unlocked it. Tāwera slipped inside, and she relocked it.

"I have less than fifteen minutes before I need to return to the store to relieve Carolyn."

"Is that food I smell? I'm starving."

Nyree led the way to the kitchen and arrived just as the microwave pinged. "It's the leftover stew from last night's dinner. There's enough for you." As she spoke, she pulled out two bowls and dished up the stew.

Tāwera grabbed eating utensils along with butter and plates without her asking him while she heated two rolls she'd taken from the freezer. They sat together and started eating.

"I don't have a photo of Ari. I deleted them off my phone."

"Is there an online one you can show me? From that social media place?"

Nyree scanned her watch and stood. "I'm sure there is one, but the internet is down at present. I'll try again later tonight." She picked up their dirty dishes.

"Leave them," Tāwera said. "I can clean the kitchen for you. You return to work."

Nyree smiled her thanks. "I'll see you later." She leaned over and kissed him on the lips. She'd intended a quick kiss, but their lips clung together, and their tongues tangled. Nyree forced herself to step back, her breathing fast and choppy. "Tonight."

"Tonight," Tāwera agreed.

Nyree paused on her doorstep, looking both ways first. When she spotted nothing to alarm her, her breath eased out, and she hustled to the store.

"Perfect timing," Carolyn said. "I swear we've been busier this season than last. The visitors purchase more than they used to when I spent more time here. Oh, before I forget. There was a man in here asking after you. He said he's a friend of your sisters and promised he'd say hello."

"Oh?" Nyree controlled her reaction with difficulty, even as the rational part of her brain stated that Ari wouldn't follow her halfway across the world. While he'd never hurt for money—he'd helped himself to hers—Carolyn had told her the fares for these ships were around thirty thousand New Zealand dollars. Ari would never spend that type of money to chase her.

Of course, he wouldn't. That would make no sense.

"Did he leave a name? Was he coming back?"

"He said he was going on a walk over to Shackleton's grave and would return later."

"His name?"

"Oh, sorry. He didn't say. He said this was a surprise visit, and he wanted to see as much as he could before he left."

Nyree offered another smile. It didn't sit right on her mouth, but Carolyn seemed fine with her response. "Thanks."

"I'll see you later," Carolyn said.

Nyree nodded and got to work. Every time someone entered the store, she glanced up to see who it was, but not one familiar face arrived. Frustratingly, it was too busy to use her phone to check the social media pages. As the hour neared six, the tension in her shoulders grew.

But no one came. Instead, the passengers trickled out and returned to their ship. Relieved that her fears had been groundless, Nyree counted the day's takings and restocked her shelves.

It was seven by the time she dropped off the takings to Carolyn and noticed the ship remained.

Nyree's brows lifted. "Why is the ship still here?"

"The captain contacted us. A passenger is missing. A male. They have a search team out looking for him."

"What nationality? Do we have a name? Did they want help?"

"No, not at the moment. We don't have any details yet. All I know is that it's a man. Keith has gone down to speak with the captain."

"Has this ever happened before?"

"Not that I know of," Carolyn said. "The ship's passengers are normally good about returning to the ship on time."

"I'll go back and have something to eat. Let me know if I can do anything to help."

Carolyn sighed. "Yes, I will. I hate to think of a man lying injured somewhere. The forecast is for temperatures to drop tonight."

Nyree made her way down the rutted path, keeping her wits about her. The first thing she'd do was find Ari's picture on social media and show it to Tāwera. If Ari was somewhere in South Georgia, she wanted to know.

CHAPTER 16

Abducted

"What's wrong?" Tāwera asked as soon as Nyree stomped into the kitchen. "Should I have not cooked dinner?" He gestured at the meat simmering in her battered pot. The pungent scent of curry spices filled the room, but she ignored the enticing food.

"Give me my tablet," Nyree ordered.

Wordlessly, Tāwera handed it over, and she tapped keys and brought up one of her social media channels. She scrolled through photos. Finally, she stopped, scowling at the face on her screen. She extended the tablet to Tāwera. "Is this him? The man you saw?"

Tāwera grimaced. "It's the same man. He resembles my brother,

Rāwiri. Is this your Ari?"

"He's not my Ari," Nyree snapped. "I loathe this man. He tried to control me and treated me like a possession. He took my money. According to him, nothing I did was right."

"Why didn't you go to the people who uphold the law?"

Nyree made a scoffing sound. "The police? Ari is personable and has friends who work at the local police station. I doubt they would've believed me. Besides, I gave him access to my bank accounts. That stupidity was on me." She pulled out a wooden chair and sank onto it, the urge to cry so intense her eyes burned.

"Nyree, we can pack a bag and fly to another part of the island until the ship leaves."

She lifted her head, feeling immeasurably older. "The ship is still here because a passenger has gone missing. A male."

"This Ari has disappeared?"

"I'm not sure of the man's identity, but my gut says it's him."

"We can leave."

"No, I'm not letting Ari get to me again. I must continue my normal routine. They'll find their missing passenger—whoever they are—and they'll get him on board and leave. All I need to do is wait him out."

"How can I help?" Tāwera asked.

Nyree shrugged. "Let's eat dinner and wait to see what happens next. It smells delicious. Have you cooked meals before?"

"Never," Tāwera said. "Men of my time hunted while the

women prepared the food."

"Yet it doesn't bother you to cook now?"

"I enjoy learning new skills. You told me men cook now."

"I did, and it's true. Roles for men and women are more varied these days. I can do anything."

Tāwera served their dinners and set a plate of rice and chunky meat in a sauce before her. He joined her at the table, his expression interested. "Like what?" he asked.

"I can build houses or join our army or other armed forces. I could fly a plane or pilot a ship. Anyone can be a doctor, nurse, teacher, or lawyer. The only thing that limits us is ourselves or the lack of opportunity."

"Could I learn a new job when we get back to Aotearoa?"

"Yes."

A thump on her door had Nyree starting. They shared a glance, but neither moved until the pounding repeated.

"I'll get it," Nyree said.

Tāwera stood. "I'm coming with you."

"Stay out of sight," she warned.

Every instinct told her not to answer, but she couldn't ignore the summons either. "Who is it?"

No one replied.

She exchanged a glance with Tāwera, who moved closer to her.

"Let me," he whispered.

She hesitated, then nodded. Carolyn had seen Tāwera leave her quarters. It wasn't as if he was a secret now.

Tāwera cracked open the door. Without warning, it flew back into his face and knocked him over. A masculine body shoved his way into her quarters and slammed the door behind him. Tall and broad with black hair, familiar blue eyes, and lightly tanned skin, he locked the door, pausing to kick Tāwera in the ribs before stepping over him and focusing on her.

"Hello, Nyree. Did you think you could hide from me?"

Everything in Nyree clenched tight. Her mouth trembled before she bit down on her bottom lip to stem the tell. Ari's grin told her he'd seen, and her fear pleased him. She took a step back, retreating by habit instead of standing her ground.

"What are you doing here?" she snapped. Her gaze darted to Tāwera. He wasn't moving, hadn't made a sound.

Ari growled, full of masculine posturing. Superiority. He backhanded her before she could evade him. "Who is he? I turn my back, and you're shacked up with another man. You belong to me."

Her nostrils flared, bravery stepping up and firming her spine. Anger burst through her. Fury. She'd let him do this to her before. No more. She wiped the blood from the corner of her mouth, stared at it for brief seconds. Her head lifted, and she punched him back, not holding back her taniwha strength. "I don't belong to anyone but myself. I choose who to spend my time with, and you have no rights over me."

Ari rocked on his feet, gaping at her as he flexed his jaw. His eyes took on a strange glow. "You know, that's the first time you've shown a bit of spark. I was beginning to think I'd imagined your special powers."

Nyree lifted her chin to frown at him. "I have no idea what you're talking about." Why wasn't Tāwera moving? The collision with the door shouldn't have knocked him out, given his taniwha status.

"I followed you," Ari said. "Thought you were cheating on me. Imagine my surprise when you, your mother, and sister transformed into dragons."

"Taniwha," Nyree corrected, lifting her chin.

Ari's eyes narrowed. "You've changed, and not for the better."

Nyree sniffed. Talk about a prince. *Not.* "You haven't changed. You're still a bastard," she snapped.

Ari lunged and struck her again, darting out of the way with a nimbleness that belied his size.

Nyree's jaw ached from the first blow, and now her shoulder pulsated in concert. Bastard. If it weren't for her healing abilities, she'd be feeling a lot worse. She eyed Ari with more caution. She'd forgotten how quick and vicious he could be. Even as she thought this, he turned his gaze to Tāwera.

"Who is this? Your new boyfriend?"

Nyree ignored the question. "They're searching for you. Have you considered the other passengers? The inconvenience you're causing everyone?"

"Shut up and answer my question."

Nyree edged away, out of Ari's reach. If he followed her, he'd be farther away from Tāwera. "What do you hope to gain by this? We're miles from anywhere. It's not as if you can take me onto your cruise ship. They'll notice a new passenger."

Ari pulled a gun out of his jacket and pointed it at her. "Answer my fuckin' question. Now! Who is he?"

"My friend."

"Are you sleeping with him?"

Nyree stared at Ari while her mind worked busily. When would Tāwera move? Given his taniwha heritage, an injury shouldn't have disabled him this much.

"Are. You. Sleeping. With him?" Ari gritted out, his face contorted and the gun still pointed in her direction.

"We're not together any longer," Nyree retorted, stalling for time. Had Tāwera moved? Yes, he had. Relief filled her. At least he knew what a gun was because they'd watched a cop movie on her tablet a few days ago. "It's none of your business what I do."

"You're mine until I'm done with you," Ari gritted out.

Keep him talking. Appeal to his vanity rather than riling him any further. "What's your plan?" Nyree asked. "I take it you want me to come with you. I can't board the ship because their security people will notice."

"Do I look stupid? Of course, I have a plan."

Nyree sucked in a breath, trying to behave as naturally as she could with a gun pointed at her. Tāwera had vanished. She hadn't heard or seen him leave, but he moved like the ghost he'd once been. What did Tāwera intend to do? Her gaze took in the splotches of blood where he'd been lying. A few spots headed toward the doorway. Had he slipped outside? Gone for help? She wished she knew.

"What are you staring at?" Ari spun without warning and fired a shot at the spot where Tāwera had been lying before he registered Tāwera's disappearance. "Where did he go?"

"I don't know. I didn't see him leave."

Ari fired a shot in Nyree's direction, and she ducked instinctively.

He laughed. "I'd never shoot the golden goose."

"What are you talking about?"

"Once I discovered your special abilities, I contacted my cousin who runs our local MC. He saw us together one day and told me if I no longer wanted you, I should give you to him. He offered money to sweeten the pot."

"You're selling me?" She gaped at the crazy man, and his expression never wavered. He meant every word. She spluttered, "You can't do that."

"You'll do what I tell you, or your mother and sister will suffer."

Panic roared through Nyree before commonsense broke through her anxiety. Manu was monitoring her family. He wouldn't let anyone hurt them, and she trusted her cousin implicitly. Once he gave his word, he never broke it. She inched farther away and smiled sweetly. "I don't think so."

Ari fired again, but it was a warning shot. He didn't mind knocking her around, but he wouldn't shoot her because he needed her healthy and alive.

"You'll attract attention."

"Perhaps, but it doesn't matter. This is what's going to happen. You will come outside with me. We will sneak from the settlement to a quiet place where you can do your dragon thing. You're going to take me across to the far side of the island where my cousin will meet me with his boat."

Nyree's mouth dropped open. The dozens of flaws in his plan made it laughable. When she was in her dragon form, she could toast him with her fire or drop him deep in the mountains. He'd vanish without a trace. If he thought she'd calmly follow his instructions, he truly was ridiculous.

"How much is your cousin paying for me?"

"One million for you and your sister." He smirked at her. "Virgins are a hot commodity, and with her powers, she's worth more than you."

She'd bet anything he didn't have her mother or sister. *Not yet.* "How do you know your cousin will come with a boat?"

"He's there now. Waiting for my arrival."

"I see."

Ari chortled, and the sound held a hint of madness. "My contact is looking forward to meeting you. He wants to fuck you and breed powerful dragon offspring."

"This man believes your tall tales?"

"Bah! You admitted you were a taniwha already, and I've seen you shifting and flying with my own eyes. I have video footage, which proved useful while arranging the sale."

"Moron," she snapped, disgusted with herself for ever thinking she'd loved this man or had a future with him.

"Stop mucking around," Ari said, his voice hard and as flat as his pale eyes. "My cousin has people watching your mother and sister. Cooperate, or your mother will die."

Nyree tried to speak, but fear grew knots in her throat, preventing words from forming. She trembled even as she tried to think of a plan. She didn't believe her mother was in immediate danger, but she couldn't be certain. It wasn't as if she could check. It would take time to contact Manu. She had to believe Manu had kept her mother and sister safe.

"All right." The words emerged as a whisper instead of the snarl she'd intended.

"Nyree? What's wrong?" Tāwera's voice slid into her mind.

Relief almost took her out at the knees. She closed her eyes before realizing Ari was watching her closely. She opened her eyes and edged toward the door in the direction Ari indicated with his gun barrel.

"I'm fine. You?" There was no point telling Tāwera the truth. They needed to remain calm because she didn't trust Ari one bit.

"My head aches. Should I tell someone he is holding you at gunpoint?"

"Yes, approach the security team from the visiting ship. If you can't find them, let Carolyn or Keith know what is going on without telling them about our dragon status."

"It must remain a secret."

"Yes."

"Do as he says. We will come for you. I am an excellent tracker."

"Move!"

While she'd been concentrating on Tāwera, Ari had drifted closer. He jabbed her in the back, and a kitchen chair went flying when her foot caught the leg.

"Quiet. I'd hate to attract attention."

Idiot. Surely someone had heard the gunshots.

"I have Keith. We are talking to the ship people," Tāwera said without warning. *"They heard the gunfire and were making a plan. One of them peeked in the window and saw the man with the gun."*

"All right. Tell them it is my ex-boyfriend, and he's known for his violence. He won't hesitate to shoot if they get too close."

Tāwera fell silent, and Nyree presumed he was communicating the knowledge to the ship's crew.

"Outside," Ari gestured with the gun again. "Now."

"We're coming out," she told Tāwera.

"The security man has gone to get weapons. They thought it was a simple search and rescue, that Ari had become lost or had fallen."

"Stand out of Ari's sight. He's likely to shoot you if he gets the chance."

"What do you intend to do?"

"He wants me to fly him across the island," Nyree said. *"He seems to think I will take him without protest, but he hasn't thought through the practicalities."*

"You could flame or drop him."

"Exactly."

"That's what you should do. Walk with this Ari to a private area where the others don't see you shift. Somewhere near the church. I can shift now. You told me the bullets would not pierce dragon scales."

"Not easily."

Ari nudged her in the ribs with his gun. "Why are you dithering? Move."

Nyree sighed. "And go where?"

"Walk away from the settlement and turn into a dragon."

Nyree bit back her protest and cursed at herself. This was all her fault. Through her stupidity in hooking up with Ari, she'd placed her family and friends in danger. Ari had discovered her secret and told others. He had proof, yet he'd bided his time. He'd made one mistake, though. Once she left the settlement, she could use her full dragon strength against him. At first, she'd panicked and reverted to normal behavior—pretending to be a weak human. He still thought he could best her with his physical strength.

Wrong.

She'd get him away from the others, and once he presented no danger to anyone else, she'd go all dragon on his arse. If she couldn't beat him on the ground, she'd drop him on his head while flying over the mountains. She'd make sure he fell in a crevice where no one would ever discover his body.

"We're outside now," she told Tāwera. *"Make sure everyone knows he's carrying a loaded weapon. He's not afraid to shoot."*

Nyree pushed open the door and stepped outside. She spotted three men, but they took cover when Ari stepped out behind her, his gun visible.

"One of the security men is ex-army. He thinks he can shoot Ari from long range. They have a special gun that does this. Can you put distance between you and this man? They're afraid of hitting you in error."

"They're going to shoot?"

"The security team said he caused trouble during the trip from South America. He apologized and told them he was ashamed of himself, that he'd drunk too much alcohol and wouldn't do it again. He's behaved since, but they don't trust him."

"But to kill him..." Nyree trailed off and jerked forward three steps when Ari shoved her. That's precisely what she'd planned for Ari.

"Isn't that what you intend to do to him? This way, he dies or gets

injured, and you don't have his death on your conscience."

Nyree shot a glance at Ari. His expression held determination, but she didn't think he'd hurt her since he intended to sell her. God, her mother, and Hana. If he'd hurt them... *"All right. But let me try to talk him down again. Maybe he'll listen to reason."* She doubted it, but then she wouldn't have to explain dragons to everyone witnessing this drama.

"Ari, this is crazy."

"Keep walking," he snarled, and his tone had her stiffening. Tension threaded through it. Stress. He was about to snap because things weren't going his way.

"Ari, they have guns too. This plan of yours won't work. You can't force me to do anything."

"You'll follow my word to the letter if you want the continued safety of your mother and sister. If you want to see them again, you will follow my orders."

She hesitated because he sounded so confident.

"Where is this ship?" she asked as she started walking toward the church.

"Nyree, don't go with him," Tāwera pleaded. *"I don't trust him. He looks like my brother, and if he is as loose with his morals and the truth as Rāwiri turned out to be, he won't keep his word. He's learned your secrets and thinks to profit from them. You can't believe anything he says."*

"No," Nyree agreed. *"But I don't want anyone here to get hurt.*

We're so far away from help."

Ari pushed her again and snarled at her. "Walk, dammit."

"I'm moving. Stop shoving me around."

"You will come with me. You will fly me to the boat, or you'll never see your precious family again."

Nyree walked as slowly as she dared without drawing more of his wrath.

Once they reached the hill above the church, they were out in the open until they climbed to a higher elevation. Not even for Ari was she shifting there. She vacillated over what to do. No matter what choice she made, it was dangerous. If Keith or Carolyn, or any of the scientists spotted a dragon flying off with Ari, that would be a disaster. Carolyn had come to believe the dragon she'd seen was a figment of her exhausted imagination. Nyree wanted Carolyn to continue thinking of dragons as fictional.

They passed the church, and Nyree still dithered over her best course of action.

Ari dug his gun into her back. "I know what you're doing. Walk faster."

Nyree lengthened her strides. *"Tāwera, I don't know what to do. Tāwera?"* When he didn't reply, she glanced over her shoulder. The security team was following but maintaining their distance. They weren't sure what to do either. *"Tāwera,"* she called again. *"Where are you?"*

Complete silence greeted her, and she had never felt so alone.

CHAPTER 17

Farewell

Tāwera sprinted through the lengthening shadows toward the cemetery and rapidly climbed until he was no longer visible from the settlement or the ship moored in the harbor. His heart thumped against his ribs with a cadence noisy enough to drown out nature's sounds. Once he reached a haphazard pile of gray rocks and privacy, he stripped off his footwear and clothing and focused on centering his mind. He had to do this to help Nyree. She wasn't a killer, despite her dragon status.

Her conscience would trouble her. He knew this because he understood her.

Tāwera breathed deeply and exhaled to settle his jangling fears.

He could do this.

After another hasty breath of mountain air, Tāwera pictured his taniwha and willed his body to shift. Once again, his shift was sluggish, but this time he experienced tender muscles rather than outright pain. Not as untroubled as this morning's shift. *Okay, discomfort he could deal with today.*

The second half of his shift progressed faster than the last time. Now to fly. He needed to keep out of sight and soar up to the top of the hill where he could help Nyree escape. Together, they could best this Ari person.

Tāwera sprang upward, his wings beating faster than average to catch the air. He lifted off, the discomfort remaining. It was a peculiar ache in his bones, but at least he knew he was alive. Even better, he was flying more easily than during his outing with Nyree.

He flew over a ridge, keeping low. *"Nyree, can you hear me?"*

She didn't answer, and alarm flowed through him. Were they too far apart, or had Ari injured her?

He upped his wingbeats, the force of the wind greater against his body. The soreness increased to a low-level pain, and for an instant, panic beset him. No! He must do this for Nyree. He wanted a future with her. He wanted to grow old with her. The thought of children flashed through his mind and the prospect of what they might have fueled his determination.

Tāwera released a roar that echoed through the hills. It was a roar of resolution. His will to succeed to make this vision come true.

He swallowed back the pain and flew in the direction he thought Nyree and Ari would've walked.

"Nyree?" He tried again, and once again, silence greeted him.

His breaths emerged with a harsh rasp, his fitness lacking for this second flight of the day, but he flew onward on sheer willpower. If Ari killed Nyree or injured her, he'd never forgive himself. He soared over another hill, and his wings stilled, shock filling him at the sight of three dragons flying toward him. A black dragon like him, along with a red and a green.

He plummeted two feet before he remembered to flap his wings. Friend or foe? What did he do now?

"Tāwera?"

His name slid into his mind, the tone containing power.

"Yes," Tāwera replied with caution.

"I am Manu. With me is my cousin, Hone, and my brother, Kahurangi."

"How did you get here?" Tāwera wheezed.

"Where is Nyree?" Manu asked.

"The Ari-man has her. He wants her to shift and fly him to a boat. I was attempting to intercept them. We didn't want the humans to see either of us, but Nyree has gone silent. She is not answering."

"You are not flying strongly," Manu observed as he and the other two dragons soared at Tāwera's side.

"The curse has affected my flight ability. This way."

"Can you make it?" Manu asked, concern in his voice.

"*I must,*" Tāwera replied. "*To save Nyree.*"

"*You like her,*" Manu said.

"*Yes, very much.*"

"*How much farther?*"

"*We're almost there. We should see them at any minute.*" Tāwera kept pumping his wings, but exhaustion was taking its toll. He was sinking closer to the land. Relief struck when he spotted Nyree and Ari. "*Nyree?*"

"*Tāwera,*" she replied.

"*We're coming to save you.*"

"*We?*" A sliver of pain leaked through their mental bond, and fury propelled him onward as Ari struck her with the gun. They were now close enough to see and hear Ari's shouts and orders.

"Change to a dragon and fly me to the ship."

Nyree straightened, and confidence blazed in her. "No."

Ari slapped her so hard she fell, and with his attention riveted on her, he didn't notice the dragons silently hovering above him. Ari went to grab her, his plan obvious. He intended to beat her into submission. Nyree jerked from his touch and twisted her body, at the same time kicking out and striking his upper thigh. He let out a roar of pain and cursed.

Tāwera seized the human's inattention to attack by blasting him with flames. Ari roared and stepped back. His boot slipped on the loose scree, and he screamed in panic. His arms windmilled, and for the first time, he perceived the four dragons hovering overhead.

Ari's legs moved, but instead of saving himself, he lost his footing and toppled backward over a steep incline. There was a scream as he rolled and hit the studded rocks, then silence.

"The humans are coming," Manu warned.

"Is he alive?" Tāwera asked.

One dragon darted in the direction Ari had fallen. A minute passed before the dragon reappeared.

"If he's not dead, he's badly wounded. He has a broken leg at least, and blood has pooled around his head," the dragon reported.

"We should go," Manu said. *"Tāwera, with us."*

"Are Mum and Hana safe?" Nyree demanded.

"Yes," Manu said. *"We got word of the kidnap plot and moved them to friends in the South Island. They are safe and helping Jessalyn with her work. We'll leave now. You'll find us in King Haakon Bay, near the start of the route that Shackleton took to make his land crossing. We'll meet you there later tonight."*

Men's voices carried on the air, and Nyree nodded. "I can deal with this. Thank you for coming for me." She smiled at Tāwera and stepped close enough to kiss him on the snout. *"Manu will look after you."*

"Move out now," Manu ordered.

Tāwera doubted he had the energy, and his liftoff was not the best. He groaned inwardly, the pain a notch higher than earlier.

"Great job," Manu encouraged. *"We'll fly out of sight and let you rest. No hurry. We have the remainder of the day to travel to the ship.*

We're happy to explore on the way."

A surge of gratefulness filled Tāwera. *"Thank you."*

Four hours later, they reached the coast, and Tāwera landed on the pebbled beach with a clumsy thump, his muscles screaming in agony as he skidded across the gray stones. A group of lazing elephant seals jolted upright in alarm. The bulls postured with their prominent noses but soon gave way to the dragons. The animals lumbered to the far end of the beach at a speed Tāwera admired even as pain tormented him with each muscle twitch.

The other dragons shifted and dressed in clothes they produced from a bag. Tāwera sat where he'd landed and struggled to calm his breathing. He didn't even mind the ugly stench from the bulky seals. Each breath was a gift when every muscle in his body throbbed like an aching tooth. He wasn't sure he'd manage a shift.

"I'll grab clothes for Tāwera," one man said.

"Bring food too," Manu ordered. "Something to drink." He turned to Tāwera. "Can you shift, or do you need rest first?"

Tāwera sighed. What sort of taniwha was he? He didn't look any older than these dragons, yet he felt immeasurably senior to them.

Manu gripped his forearm before releasing it. "Can you tell me about the problems you're having? Perhaps I can help."

Tāwera explained shifting was difficult. It could be painful, although this time, he'd managed better. He became starving, and sex worked far better to counteract his moonlust than shifting.

"You and Nyree had sex."

228

"No," Tāwera snapped. *"We made love. I like and respect Nyree. I wish to have a future with her."*

"What does Nyree think about this? How did she react to the fact I thought you might be mates?"

"Mates? When did you say this?"

"When I replied to your email."

"I did not see this reply."

"I see." Something in Manu's tone had Tāwera studying him closely, and he noted the quiver of his lips.

"How did you know to come to Nyree's aid?"

"Ari wanted to sell Nyree, her mother, and her sister to the local MC club after he discovered she could shift to a dragon. Unknown to Ari, the vice president of the club is my cousin. He informed me, and we came up with a plan to help Nyree and trap Ari in a place where we could deal justice and put a stop to his plan."

"You intended to kill Ari all along?"

"He beat Nyree and threatened her family. Our people. That is not acceptable."

"No, it isn't," Tāwera agreed. *"She allowed him to beat her to protect those she cared for."*

"I understand that now," Manu said. "She should've come to me earlier, so I could help her. We thought she'd be safe here, but I underestimated Ari's determination. Nyree's departure pricked his pride, and he wanted to punish her for the slight."

"You understand him. He bears an uncanny resemblance to my

brother, although his skin is much paler than Rāwiri's. Half-brother. The one who placed the curse on me."

"You think Ari is a descendant of your brothers?"

"It is possible since you told me my brother married and had several children with Aroha."

"The woman you were to marry."

"Yes," Tāwera said. "I was young then. What I feel for Nyree is very different to those I had for Aroha."

"Glad to hear it. Ah, here is Hone with clothes for you. Do you think you can shift now?"

"I must," Tāwera said.

"I have a few theories about your shifting problems. We will talk later. It might be best if you eat something first while you are in dragon form, then attempt to shift."

"Very well."

Tāwera ate strips of meat Hone tossed him and drank a bowl of water. The rest and the food helped. Although, he still had to grit his teeth to contain his pained bellows while he shifted. He emerged from his dragon form in a shaky heap, his legs refusing to hold his weight.

Manu helped him to stand and handed him a pile of clothes. "You have a full facial moko. You were a warrior?"

"Yes," Tāwera said. "I understand this will make integrating difficult for me, but I still wish to try."

The three men glanced at each other before turning back to him.

"You will fit in fine," Manu assured him. "We will find a position that suits your interests and skills. We'll speak with Nyree before we leave, but I think she'll agree with our plan."

Tāwera enjoyed the men's company. Manu and Hone had mates, while Kahurangi had a casual girlfriend. He learned of their jobs, their lives, and told them more of what had happened to him.

There were other men on the boat, but none of them approached them. It raised Tāwera's curiosity, but he wasn't standing close enough to do a sniff test to ascertain their race.

"These other sailors. Do they know you're taniwha?" he asked.

"They're taniwha too—a fishing crew from near Wellington."

Tāwera frowned. "I do not know this place."

"It is our capital city and lies at the bottom of the North Island. The crew are water dragons and have an affinity for the sea."

"Ah! I have heard of water dragons but never met one. There were none where I lived in Northland."

"We were lucky they intended to come down south for a jaunt. From there, it was easy to arrange with our contacts at the MC club to use us to pick up Ari and Nyree."

Tāwera nodded. "Ari thought he'd arranged the boat when it was you. What will we do next? What if Ari is not dead, or if he has told someone we cannot control?"

"Nyree will let us know Ari's fate," Manu said. "There's no point worrying until we learn what has happened to him. Once we have her report, we can plan from there."

Tāwera had read several of Manu's emails. He'd known Nyree respected her tribal leader, but the more he spoke with him, the more Tāwera understood what a great man he was and how lucky he was to have Manu's help.

Nyree arrived during their dinner. She landed with a bag clutched in her talons, and Tāwera shot to his feet. Despite the pain still pounding his muscles, he reached her in three long strides. He waited impatiently for her to shift and pull on her clothes before he yanked her into his arms.

He held her and breathed in her floral scent. "Are you injured?"

She hugged him back. "I'm fine. A few bruises and sore parts, but I heal fast."

"Ari?"

"He's dead. He was alive when they hauled him up the cliff, but he died while receiving medical attention from the ship's doctor."

Relief swept Tāwera. "Did anyone see us in our dragon form?"

"No. We're safe." She pushed away from Tāwera and threaded her fingers with his before she turned to Manu and the others. "Excellent timing. I didn't realize you were heading this way."

"The plan came together fast. Once we realized Ari's scheme, we kept him under surveillance and acted accordingly."

Nyree sniffed. "You didn't think to clue me in on your plan? You kept me waiting for ages for replies to my emails. I didn't hear a word about you heading my way."

"We didn't want Ari to become suspicious, nor did we wish to panic you. We've been here a couple of days waiting for his arrival. Once we knew the timing, we planned to stake out the settlement. The trouble was getting close enough to spy on Ari without being seen. He's met each of us through you, which meant we had to keep out of sight."

"At least you arrived in time to help."

"I didn't realize he'd come out with you at gunpoint. Made things a mite tricky. We'll take Tāwera home to New Zealand with us," Manu stated in a change of subject.

Nyree blinked, an immediate protest springing to her lips. She swallowed hard, her glance darting to Tāwera. She found his gaze trained on her, his expression serious.

"I guess that's the best idea," she said, trying not to sound reluctant.

"Nyree, Tāwera has no papers. No passport. If he goes back with us, we can come in close to shore and fly home. It's safer for Tāwera."

Nyree nodded, but she hated him leaving. They'd known each other for a short time, yet she'd fallen for him. He was her friend, her... "That's a great idea," she forced herself to say.

"There's food left if you're hungry," Manu said.

"I could eat." Nyree stood to grab a plate from the makeshift rock table.

Manu reached out and placed a hand on her shoulder. She jerked upright at the wash of power that radiated from him and filtered into her arm. "It's obvious you care for one another. Tāwera knows nothing of our world. He needs to see New Zealand as it is now and visit his home. He needs time to find his place and decide what he wants to do. If he comes with us now, we won't have to worry about identification papers straightaway."

"I wouldn't get in the way or stop him from doing anything," Nyree whispered.

Manu's mouth twisted. "That's not what I'm saying. You're good together—from what I've seen. Tāwera was a warrior. He's used to making decisions and acting decisively. Consider his pride, his position. His *mana*. The months apart will also tell you if your friendship could be more."

"You've made your decision. Nothing I say will make you change your mind." Her words sounded reluctant. Selfish.

"I'm an outsider looking in," Manu said, squeezing her shoulder in commiseration. "It's easier for me to see what will work best because I'm not emotionally involved."

"We're friends. That's all." A pang pierced her chest once her words settled. She closed her eyes briefly before risking a glance at Manu. He wore his regular patient expression as he waited for her to say more.

She sighed. "No, that's not true. I feel more than friendship for Tāwera, but it's not fair to him. He should experience this world and meet other people. Other women."

Manu leaned closer and hugged her. "And that's why I think everything will work out all right."

Nyree sighed again, this time internalizing the confusion and unwillingness to let Tāwera go with Manu. She didn't have a choice, and it was heartless of her even to want to keep him with her. He'd spent hundreds of years cursed and contained within the stone she'd discovered. It was time for him to embrace his freedom, and he couldn't do that here in South Georgia.

She released Manu and rose. "I'll say goodbye."

She formed her lips into a smile and kept her false bravado pasted in place as she approached Tāwera and the others, the gray pebbles shifting beneath her bare feet. "How are you? You managed the flight across the island all right?"

"Some pain and I'm exhausted. I doubt I could get off the ground now, but it wasn't as difficult as last time."

Nyree nodded. "Manu and the others will help you figure out why flying is so painful for you. They'll organize identification papers and everything else you need."

"Ari is dead."

"Yes."

"He was a relation," Tāwera said.

"We don't know that for sure." Nyree lifted her chin, renewed anger at Ari flooding her. "And we aren't to blame for his death."

"That's one thing we'll do when we get back home," Hone said, obviously overhearing. "My father is the expert in genealogy. Does Ari have a family?"

"A younger sister. His parents are still alive, but they live in Australia on the Gold Coast," Nyree said. "What were you thinking?"

"A DNA test," Hone said. "Compare Tāwera's DNA with Ari's sister's. The man who resembled Ari was half-brother to Tāwera. At least that way, you might trace family members."

"Family is important," Tāwera said, wincing as he shrugged his shoulders. He prodded his biceps and pulled a face, stretching gingerly.

Nyree picked up a plate and grabbed fresh salad, ham, and bread to make a sandwich. She focused on the food, not letting her mind dart into the pain she was experiencing at the thought of Tāwera's departure.

All too soon, it was time to go.

"We'll let you say your goodbyes in private," Manu said.

He, Hone, and Kahurangi packed up their food and trash and carried their inflatable boat down the beach, past a hovering group of curious king penguins, to the water.

"My cousins will look after you," Nyree said. "Ask questions if anything confuses you or if you require advice. All of them are decent men. Hone's father, George, is also an excellent person to approach. Manu will introduce you to our families and friends. You will fit in with the others. You learn fast." To her horror, tears dampened her eyes. She blinked hard to barricade them in position.

Tāwera pursed his lips. "You are sad."

"I'll miss you," Nyree blinked several times.

"We will email," Tāwera promised. "I will tell you all that I am doing."

Nyree stepped forward to embrace him, but Tāwera had other ideas. Yes, he drew her close, but he kissed her on the lips, taking his time and making it a kiss to remember. When Tāwera stepped back, her tears were under control, and her pulse was racing. She sensed her cousins' interest, but she ignored them and smiled.

"Behave," she said lightly. "Have fun."

"I will see you soon, Nyree." Tāwera beamed at her, then stalked away to join the other men. They pulled the inflatable into deeper water and clambered inside. The last thing she saw of Tāwera was his hand raised in farewell as they scrambled up an iron ladder to board the fishing boat.

Nyree stayed until the ship motored out of the bay, and it rounded the corner and disappeared. The thickness in her throat stirred again, and tears blurred her vision. Longing flooded her, yet she remained still and silent.

Her heart went with Tāwera.

CHAPTER 18

Home Again

Nyree arrived back at Grytviken almost two hours later with dusk about to fall. She'd taken her camera with her and snapped photos of craggy mountain peaks and hidden bays to show Carolyn and Keith if they asked questions.

They'd expressed concern after her ordeal and pondered the wiseness of exploring tonight. She'd assured them she was well but needed time alone to recover and regain her serenity. Photography always calmed her. Although she was back on time, she'd prepared if either of them interrogated her.

"There you are," Carolyn said, concern and relief shimmering in her voice. She brushed a dark brown curl away from her eyes as she studied Nyree. What she saw must've reassured her. "I wondered if you and your scientist would like to come for dinner tomorrow night."

Nyree grimaced and sought a credible lie. "We argued. It turns out he has a wife back in New Zealand he didn't tell me about."

Renewed concern filled Carolyn's face. "Nyree, I'm so sorry. After everything that happened today with your ex-boyfriend too."

"I don't seem to have much luck with men."

"Come to dinner anyway. The captain of the cruise ship sent us three bottles of wine. We might open one to have with dinner."

Nyree hesitated before deciding to agree to the suggestion. At least Carolyn and Keith would stop her moping. "Thanks. That sounds lovely. Do you want me to bring anything?"

"Just yourself," Carolyn said, patting her hand. "I thought we'd change the museum displays tomorrow morning since we don't have a ship in port until one in the afternoon. Are you up for that?"

"I prefer to keep busy."

"See you bright and early in the morning. We'll start at eight. Good night. Oh, before I forget. Keith said the Falklands police want to talk to you about Ari. Keith will organize the call for tomorrow."

Nyree shuddered. "What did they do with his body?"

"They took him to the morgue on board the cruise ship. They'll drop him at the Falkland Islands en route to South America."

Nyree nodded. "See you in the morning."

She wandered to her quarters and unlocked the door. Inside, the place seemed empty without Tāwera, but his presence remained. His clothes still hung in the wardrobe. The books he'd been reading sat in a haphazard pile beside his favorite chair. He'd find New Zealand very different from his memories. He'd meet people.

Women.

She sank into a chair with a sigh. Tāwera's chair, and it smelled like him. Masculine with a hint of green and the outdoors.

Two months to go before she returned to New Zealand. Plenty of time for Tāwera to meet other women. More attractive women who didn't possess the same flaws as her.

The tears she'd been holding back since she'd said goodbye to Tāwera escaped and flowed down her cheeks. A sob echoed in the air. None of this was fair, yet she couldn't fault Tāwera. It was her.

She'd informed him their time together was temporary—a friend with benefits deal—so she had no one to blame but herself.

Perhaps he wouldn't hook up with a woman?

Nyree discarded that idea straightaway. Tāwera was a handsome and memorable man. He was strong and masculine, but he listened to others. He was a protector. A warrior. He also bore a curiosity that would compel him to explore his new world.

Yes, there was no way he wouldn't meet other women, most of them without her baggage and way more attractive. He had the type of *mana* that would draw others to him, and she could see him making a success of whatever he tried.

And she was making this worse.

She had to treat her time with Tāwera as a gift, and if he still wanted to see her on her return, she could count herself lucky to have scored a friend.

The two months passed slowly without Tāwera. Nyree had her usual busy, full-on days when they had lots of cruise passengers ashore, and as the days crept toward the end of the season, the number of visiting ships decreased.

At first, she received a weekly email from Tāwera detailing everything he was doing. His excitement came through when he discovered his official relationship with Ari through Tāwera's half-brother. He'd met Eve, Ari's sister, and liked her very much, and she was talking about taking Tāwera to Australia to introduce him to her parents. Eve intended to move to Australia.

Nyree's stomach fell at this news.

That bombshell was in the latest email she'd received almost three weeks ago. Other emails contained info about the people he'd met and the places he'd visited. Manu and Jessalyn had driven him around Auckland, and Tāwera had spent time with Hone at George Taniwha & Sons.

"I can't believe the season has almost ended," Carolyn said, dragging Nyree from her morbid thoughts.

"We've had lots of excitement," Nyree agreed. "Do you think the big iceberg will hit South Georgia?"

"I don't know. You heard the scientists who are studying the iceberg mention that the evidence points to this happening before. It's a bit of a waiting game. We'll pray the ocean current veers it off its present trajectory."

"I recognize some of the penguins that hang around the station. I hate to think of them dying or having to move elsewhere because of the iceberg affecting their food source."

Carolyn shrugged. "It's nature."

"That doesn't make it any easier. What's on the schedule this morning?" Nyree asked, changing the subject.

"We need to do a stocktake. Basically, we'll note everything we have, look to see what isn't selling, and offer a discount to move the remaining units. Normally, we don't do this, but they're talking about selling different things next year. Are you coming back next season? Keith and I would love to have you as part of our team."

"To be honest, I have thought little about next year. When is the last day for applications?"

"I'll check with Keith. I think you enjoy living here, though. Many people find it too isolated."

"I'll give it some thought. The principal reason I took the job was to escape my ex. That didn't work out too well for me."

"He's in the past. You're a lovely girl, and any man would be lucky to win your loyalty."

"*Huh!* That's the problem. My judgment is lousy."

"I thought that until I met Keith. You're still young. You have time to find a husband and have children."

"*Hmm,*" Nyree said. "Do you have a special way of doing a stocktake?"

She and Carolyn settled into work and soon had the stock sorted and counted.

Nyree used the last weeks to explore the island and take lots of photos. She'd heard from her mother and Hana. Jessalyn had hired her mother as a housekeeper while Hana helped a local vineyard during the weekends, now that she was older.

They seemed much happier and were following more outside interests, which made Nyree smile. It also made her realize how domineering Ari had been over their lives and hers. No longer.

Her mother and Hana were thriving under Manu and Jessalyn's care.

The moment she woke, Nyree checked her email, hoping for one from Tāwera. There was nothing, and fear licked through her veins. She made a cup of tea and dressed. There was a noticeable chill in the wind now, and when she walked outside, she noted the higher mountains on the horizon had a fresh coating of snow.

Winter was on its way.

She made her way past the penguin colony. Most of the chicks were fully-fledged now, their feathers resembling an adult's and waterproof instead of their previous wooly brown coats. She snapped several photos, thought of home and Tāwera, and issued her usual sigh.

Tāwera had a different life now, and she was turning into a miserable, whining cow. What she needed was a plan for her return home. She had a few days in Ushuaia before she flew to Buenos Aires. After three days of sightseeing, she was catching a direct flight to New Zealand.

She had a job waiting for her back at George Taniwha & Sons but wondered if she shouldn't try a fresh start. Maybe do a little traveling in New Zealand now that her mother and sister had settled. She could learn to make coffee and work in a cafe or take a job in a bar while seeing the country.

She'd catch up with Tāwera to make certain he was happy before she moved on with her new life. During the ten-hour flight back to New Zealand, she'd make a list and decide her future.

Late March, Auckland, New Zealand

Nyree's plane ended up delayed for eight hours, and it was late afternoon by the time her Air New Zealand flight landed. With the packed aircraft, it took ages for her to deplane and collect her luggage.

Of course, the lines through immigration and customs were long and full of rude, snappish men and women who wanted to leave the airport as desperately as her.

An hour and a half later, she plodded into the public part of the airport, dragging her single bag after her. She'd emailed her arrival time to her mother and expected her mum or Hana to greet her.

Not a single welcoming face stood waiting in the terminal.

She checked her phone to find a text from her sister. Both she and her mother were working. Could she grab a cab home?

Sighing, Nyree threaded through the now smiling passengers greeting their friends and family. Outside, it was raining in the way it often did in Auckland, making the buildings appear dull and dingy. She joined the line for the cabs, also long. *Go figure.*

"Nyree!" a masculine voice called. "The traffic was terrible. We almost missed you."

Nyree blinked at the confident man striding up to her. Even dressed in jeans and a T-shirt, his long black hair loose, he oozed power and attracted glances. Before she could catalog more, he drew her in for a kiss. For an instant, she froze, shocked, and her brain took long seconds to jolt back into gear. Not understanding any of this, she just enjoyed the moment. She leaned into Tāwera and kissed him back, reveling in the physical contact and not caring they were blocking the line from advancing.

Finally, Tāwera pulled back, his grin wide on his familiar

tattooed face. Other people continued to stare, but it might have been because of his vibrant personality and the sheer happiness spilling from him. He commandeered her suitcase and clasped her hand in his free one. "Come on. Manu came with me to pick you up. He's waiting in the car park."

Bemused, Nyree walked at Tāwera's side, her mind crazy with a blur of thoughts. What was going on? She was awake because the rain was dampening her face. Tāwera had emailed her a few times, but they'd tailed off, and she'd honestly thought he'd moved on without her. But this...this was something else.

"We're this way," Tāwera said. "Your plane was late. Do you know what happened to it?"

"They had to replace a part before take-off," Nyree said.

Tāwera led her to an SUV and loaded her gear in the rear.

"Hi, Nyree," Manu said from the passenger seat. "Good flight?"

"The actual flight was okay, but everyone was grumpy because of the delay. I'm glad to be here."

Tāwera opened the rear door for her and waited until she'd settled herself before he climbed behind the wheel.

"You're driving?" she blurted.

"Yes, I have my learner's license." Tāwera's gaze met hers in the rearview mirror. "I am an excellent driver. Manu taught me."

"I see," Nyree said, glancing at a grinning Manu. An understatement. None of this meeting was going as she'd suspected.

Manu laughed outright. "Tāwera is a fantastic driver. You'll see. You should be proud of him. He has mastered many tasks."

"I have a job," Tāwera said, and pride filled his voice as he started the vehicle and pulled away from their parking space.

Nyree held her breath, tension sinking to her passenger-driver feet.

She prepared to brake then discovered Tāwera drove with a natural deftness and competence. He pulled up at the barrier arm and was soon zooming south to Papakura. Nyree relaxed another increment.

"What sort of job do you have?"

"I work for Manu and do many things," Tāwera said, leaving Nyree none the wiser.

"Did you visit your home?"

"Yes," Tāwera said. "Russell or *Kororāreka*, as I once knew it, is much changed. During my time there, it used to be a busy port, and it was the first true European settlement in Aotearoa. Now, it is a sleepy town."

"Did you find any family apart from Eve?"

"The descendants of Rāwiri. I have not told them the truth. Manu suggested I tell them I discovered a common DNA when I was searching my family history."

"That worked because we got Tāwera's DNA tested and waited to learn if he had any close connections," Manu said. "We've discovered close relations and many more distant."

"I have also searched through old documents and church records to learn what happened to my father and other people I knew. Rāwiri was a very famous tattooist. I hope no other man crossed him and ended up cursed."

"We'll probably never know, although we could search records to learn if any other men or women disappeared around the same time. We tracked down an early newspaper that noted Tāwera's abrupt departure from *Kororāreka*," Manu said. "It mentioned Aroha and how Rāwiri comforted her in her grief."

Tāwera snorted as he merged with the motorway traffic. "We know why he comforted her. Aroha was his plan all along."

Tāwera drove them to Manu's house. Manu got out there. "See you tomorrow," he said to Tāwera and disappeared inside.

Tāwera backed out of the driveway and drove farther down the road. He pulled onto a private driveway and navigated the rutted track before pulling up in front of a tidy, white bungalow. Flowers bloomed at the front of the house, giving splashes of purple and red against the white of the exterior.

"This is my home. I rent it from Manu. Your mother and sister live nearby. They are away at present, which is why I volunteered to collect you." He stopped the vehicle. "You're staying with me today. Longer if you wish. We have much to discuss."

No kidding. Nyree stared at him. So many questions. *So many questions.*

He opened the vehicle door for her, and she scrambled into

action.

"I can't wait to show you my home. I have worked hard to make it a place you would like. Come. This way. I shall collect your bag later."

Bemused, Nyree let Tāwera urge her to the front entrance. He produced a key from his pocket and unlocked the door. He stood back and ushered her inside.

By habit, Nyree slipped off her shoes before entering.

He guided her straight into an open-plan living room. The kitchen was white and spotless with all the usual contents. The lounge contained a combination of Tāwera's Māori heritage in carvings and the cushions and that of European—a blend that genuinely worked together.

As Tāwera guided her through his home, she became increasingly off-balance. She thought... But maybe...

A shudder worked down her spine, and it wasn't one of fear but more akin to moonlust, which was crazy since the full moon wasn't for another two weeks.

"I have two bedrooms," Tāwera said to her, stopping at the first. "You can use this one."

Her heart sank, and she realized she'd been kidding herself. She wanted Tāwera, and it was going to be hell to step back and let another woman scoop him up. Wait! Her thoughts skidded to an appalled halt.

That was her when she'd been with Ari. She'd let him walk all over her to hide her otherness. She'd promised herself she'd never do that again—let a man have that sort of power. It was possible to have an equal partnership. Her friends with their mates were all proof of that.

"Nyree?"

Belatedly, she realized she'd drifted into her thoughts—a product of spending much of her time alone during the last two months. "Sorry. I didn't sleep on the plane."

"I asked if you wanted this room," Tāwera said, "or you can share mine. Either choice is fine, but my preference is for you to sleep with me. I have missed you." His gaze was solemn.

"I've missed you too." She closed the distance between them. "I will share your room."

Tāwera beamed at her. "Excellent. Would you like to sleep now?"

Nyree placed her hands on his broad shoulders and took in his handsome face with the sweeping curls of his *moko*, his black hair, and his broad smile. "I would like to take a shower since I've been in these clothes for too long. Then I might go to bed, but I don't wish to sleep."

"No?" His brows rose, and she couldn't make out if he understood her meaning or not.

She spelled out her desires. "I'd like you to lie with me and give me a hug or two. Naked hugs."

CHAPTER 19

What of the Future?

Tāwera smiled so wide it hurt his mouth. "I worried you wouldn't like me as much, that we might've grown apart."

Nyree pressed a soft kiss to his mouth, her eyes shining as if she wanted to cry while her lips smiled. He thought it was happy emotion, but he found it better to ask because he didn't always pick up on social cues. "I am becoming better at reading people, but men and women differ from my time. Manu told me this is because we value different things and have more opportunities now. We can travel as you did on a plane. I wish to do that one day, but I must wait until my passport arrives. Are you happy? I can't tell."

"I am thrilled. These tears are happy ones."

Tāwera hesitated, impatience simmering through him. He knew his mind, and he preferred to govern his future with positivity rather than remaining unsure. "Since I left you in South Georgia, I have been thinking about my future. The first thing that came to my head was you. I wish to have you standing at my side."

"I *am* standing at your side."

"No, you misunderstand. I want marriage. With you. You are a good person, and you are beautiful. You saved me from the curse and gave me a second chance at life."

She tugged from his loose embrace and took a step back. "My saving you didn't come with obligations."

Ah, he hadn't explained well enough. He placed his hands on her shoulders and smiled. "I love you. I wish to share my life with you, and at a later time, have children. Say you'll step into the future with me, Nyree."

For long seconds, she remained stiff in his arms, her eyes stormy and uncertain. Then she relaxed. "Are you sure? You might change your mind."

"My mind is positive. I hope to explore this unknown world with you. I want to stay at your side and grow old with you."

"It will be a long life if you change your mind. Taniwha live longer than humans."

He met her eyes as he caressed her cheek. "If you're trying to frighten me, you're doing a poor job."

Nyree snorted and turned her face into his hand, nuzzling his fingers and palm.

His heart flip-flopped before it resettled and continued with its regular beat. "Manu believes you and I are mates. His theory is our lives can still diverge because we come from different times, but the more days and months we spend together, the tighter the connection will become. He believes this is why I have missed you so much."

Nyree met his gaze directly. "I ached for you, but I also missed your company and our talks."

"It was the same with me." Manu had also been correct when he'd told Tāwera he'd need to talk to explain himself rather than act. Tāwera had never spoken like this with Aroha and bared what was in his heart. "You are my heart, my soul, my very breath, and I am a better man when I'm with you."

Nyree raised on tiptoe and silenced his next words with her mouth. Her fingers crept behind his head and anchored him. Not that he wanted to move. He was right where he wanted to be.

When their lips parted, they were both breathing hard.

"Shower," he said. "Are you hungry?"

"Yes," she said, sounding surprised.

"Go. I shall bring food, and we will speak a little more before we have those naked hugs." His pulse jumped as his mind leaped ahead.

Manu had told him he must explain the sexual aspect of

his moonlust, that Nyree must know the entire truth, so she understood what their future entailed. He strode into his compact kitchen, taking pleasure in the clean counters and the abundance of food in his pantry and fridge.

Earlier, before Nyree's arrival, he'd asked Emma and Jessalyn what he should get to make Nyree a celebration dinner. They'd informed him she'd probably not want an enormous meal but guided him toward cheese and crackers and fruit along with a nice bottle of wine. Bubbles, they'd called it, and shown him how to open the bottle. They'd given him other advice too, which upon reflection, he'd decided was perfect.

Honesty.

Determination.

Romance.

Operation Nyree was underway, and she wouldn't stand a chance.

Nyree stepped under the warm water with a sigh of relief. Her body ached after sitting for ten hours, and she hadn't slept well for several nights, her mind full of Tāwera and what she'd find here in New Zealand on her arrival.

He loved her.

She hugged the sizzle of happiness and hurried through her shower. Five minutes later, she was drying herself.

"There is a robe hanging on the back of the door," Tāwera called down the passage. "Use that."

She pulled the black robe off the hook and slipped it on. It smelled of Tāwera, and the bit of remaining anxiety released. He'd told her he loved her. He'd missed her as much as she'd ached for his presence.

Nyree padded from the bathroom toward the kitchen. Tāwera had the radio playing, and he sang to a tune she didn't know.

"There you are." He beamed at her, his open joy tugging at her emotions.

She smiled again, anticipation thrumming through her as he spoke.

"What would you like to drink? I have water, juice, wine, beer, or I have learned how to make leaf tea. Your arrival is a celebration. I think we should have the special wine Emma and Jessalyn helped me choose. It will go with the food I have prepared." He gestured at the table. It bore three kinds of cheese—blue, cheddar, and brie—nuts and grapes, along with fresh bread and a small bowl of pickle or relish.

"Wine, it is. Where shall I sit?"

"Here." Tāwera pulled out a chair for her, and she sat.

"This reminds me of our picnic after you turned visible."

"Yes. We must talk."

"About what?"

"Moonlust."

He produced a bottle of bubbles and opened it with a professionalism that had her mouth hanging open. Tāwera poured the wine into flutes and handed her one.

"A toast." He lifted his glass. "To us and the future. Our future."

"To us and our future," she repeated. "What about moonlust?"

"My moonlust differs from yours." His brown eyes studied her reaction.

It was his scrutiny that had tension rising to settle on her shoulders. "How is it different?"

"With me, to control my taniwha, I must have sex. Flying at the full moon is only possible after I have a regular sexual release."

Suspicion came to the fore, and her knuckles whitened as she squeezed her flute. She set it on the table, not wanting to break the glass and spray champagne in all directions. "How did you cope after you arrived here?" Her pulse raced while she waited for his reply, and she tried to rein in her imagination.

"Ah! Manu said it was most important for our relationship that I tell you everything."

Nyree swallowed hard. Could she forgive him if he'd used another woman to sate his moonlust? She'd witnessed the pain he'd suffered while trying to fly. She could hardly blame him—no, she had to listen and give him a chance. If Manu had advised him, perhaps her brain had jumped to overdrive.

"After Manu and I worked out what the problem was, he suggested I find an agreeable woman to help me."

Nyree stared, waiting to hear more, even as she dreaded the truth. Despite his strength and abilities, he still had an innocent quality about him.

"I couldn't do that when you filled my mind. That would not be right. I told Manu this, which made him positive we were mates."

"What did you do? How did you get through the full moon?"

"I thought of you and used my hand. It was not the same as holding you in my arms."

Nyree frowned. "Did Manu think this would pass? Did you try shifting as well?"

"Manu has never seen or heard of this problem before. He thinks the curse interfered with my taniwha. The flight was more painful than the one after we were together. Nyree, I can read your fear. If you have any doubts, we can wait before we love each other. I will cope by myself and refuse to force you to act against your will. I am not like Rāwiri or Ari."

His instant offer and his willingness to wait blasted away her lingering doubts.

"This looks delicious. Which is your favorite cheese?"

"I like this one." He pointed to the brie. "Shall I cut you some?"

"I see you've developed a liking for French cheese and champagne."

"It reminds me of my time on the ship when I was still ghostlike.

I had a delicious meal aboard the French cruise ship."

Nyree laughed. "Our picnic that day was tasty too." She sipped her wine and savored the faint tickle of bubbles on her palate. Tāwera handed her a plate with a selection of bread, a sliver of fruit paste, and a chunk of brie.

While they ate, Tāwera told her some of what he'd done since arriving in New Zealand.

"Manu had to grasp my arm to stop me from fleeing when I first saw the roads with all the traffic."

"But you have learned to drive."

"I wanted to make you proud."

Nyree took his hand and squeezed. "I was proud of you before you left South Georgia. Few people would cope with these changes as well as you have."

"That is what Manu told me."

"What do you do for Manu?"

"I am teaching some of his tribe to carve and create items we made as warriors. Weapons and other carvings. While I was not a master, I am competent. Manu says the old ways are attractive to some, and it is a way of keeping the culture alive."

Nyree listened to Tāwera speak of his teaching and his work for George Taniwha & Sons. His enthusiasm shone through.

"Jessalyn says I should teach the traditional *haka* we used to do before going to war."

"Do you remember them?"

He nodded. "It seems like yesterday to me. We will have plenty of time to talk." He stood and held out his hand.

Nyree set down her flute and stood. She didn't take his hand but jumped at him. His arms drew her close, and it felt like coming home. His warmth and scent surrounded her as he walked down the passage to his bedroom.

"Wow," she said as she took in the contents of his bedroom—the enormous bed with the sage-green covers. The pieces of furniture were bold and heavy with beautiful flowers and vines carved into the dark wood. Two paintings—one of forest and the other of the sea—hung on the walls.

A large wardrobe took up one wall, the three sliding doors allowing access.

"I have a small bathroom through that door." Tāwera set her on the bed. "Do you like it?"

"Yes, it's beautiful."

"I thought you would. Jessalyn helped me to choose furnishings." He unbuttoned his shirt while he spoke. "I bought the pictures when I visited Russell. They were the first big things I purchased by myself. I like them because they remind me of home." He removed his jeans next and the plain black boxer-briefs he wore beneath, standing before her without shame.

"I love looking at you," she whispered. "You're an attractive man."

"Who has eyes for no one but you," he said, his gaze full of honesty.

Nyree smiled and stood, letting the robe fall to the floor in a puddle of silk.

"You are the beautiful one," he whispered. "Come here."

She walked into his arms and offered her lips. He claimed them, kissing her with more hunger than earlier. His arms curled around her, firm and determined.

"Nyree," he whispered. "I have counted the days until I could hold you again."

A sense of rightness engulfed her, and she softened, letting him lift her and place her on the bed. He came down over her, caging her within his arms, yet making her feel protected and loved.

She ran her fingertips over his cheek, skimming the old scars of his tattoos. "Tāwera," she whispered. "I didn't think I'd ever want a man after the way Ari treated me. Then you came along, and I haven't caught my breath since."

His dark brows arched. "Is that a good thing?"

A laugh burst from her. "It's perfect. That's what I'm trying to say in a roundabout way. You sneaked into my heart when I wasn't looking. I love you and can't imagine being with any other man. It's the way you view the world, your courage in attacking the unknown, your honesty and goodness. I love you more than I can describe."

"I hoped this was so, but now can we continue to ease the pain in my muscles?"

Nyree gasped. "You're in pain? Why didn't you tell me?"

"Because I don't want your sympathy. I loathe the idea of you having sex because you feel sorry for me. If that were the case, I'd prefer you to sleep in the spare room."

"Stop." Nyree placed her hand over his mouth. "Hush. This is not a pity fuck, Tāwera. Never a pity fuck. I meant it. I love you and want to be with you because you're special. All right?"

He stared at her for a fraction longer and flashed a quick smile. "We both have doubts. It will take time for us to become comfortable again."

"No, it won't," Nyree said. "The moment I walked into your home... No, it was the moment I saw you at the airport that I finally felt whole again. I won't change my mind. We have a future together, and that is final."

"Yes," Tāwera said, and he settled in to kiss her again.

This time his kiss flared full of passion, igniting a fire inside her.

Their hands wandered and explored, learning each other all over again.

She stroked his shoulders and traced fingers over his cursed tattoo that curled from his back around to the side of his rib cage. He shivered, and she lowered her head to follow the path of her fingers with her tongue.

"Nyree," Tāwera whispered, his eyes closed, and his body tensed.

"Are you ticklish?"

"No."

She backed up, moving down his body, suddenly realizing what his problem was when his cock poked her in the leg.

"Ah. I can fix this problem for you. We have all night."

Tāwera gasped as she wrapped her hands around his shaft. "M-Manu suggested I should let you sleep after your long journey."

"My cousin had a lot to say for himself," she said dryly.

"He is my friend. I trust him."

Her pique faded as fast as it had arrived. "Manu is a fine man and an excellent leader. You could not have a better friend."

"Yes." He jumped as she replaced her fingers with her lips. "Nyree," he whispered.

She took him deeper into her mouth, using her hands at the base of his shaft to control the depth of his penetration. When she pulled back, she smiled. "Just enjoy."

"But you—"

"Later," she said firmly, and she licked and stroked and sucked until her big man shuddered in her arms. His hips jerked, driving him deeper, and he groaned.

"Nyree!" he cried out seconds before he came.

She continued, kissing and stroking as she swallowed, pleasure filling her too since this was something she could give him to ease his pain. Finally, she slid back from his softened cock and crawled up the bed to kiss him. He rolled without warning, trapping her beneath him, and she groaned in anticipation. He cupped her breasts and squeezed her nipples in the way he'd learned she enjoyed. His hands stroked her body, and he kissed her lips, her neck, the curve of her breasts until she writhed beneath him.

He kissed down her body, finding every sensitive place with his lips and tongue. Her pulse raced, and pleasure roared through her, each delicious touch driving her higher. Tāwera parted her legs and nibbled on the soft flesh of her inner thighs. The next moment, he licked along her slit, and her eyes flew open, her body jolting in pleased surprise.

Tāwera's smile was slow and sexy, and it warmed her through from her head to the tips of her toes.

"Do it again," she whispered, expectation lodged low in her belly.

Satisfaction settled on his face, and he bent to do her bidding. "This spot." He licked along an edge, barely hitting her clit. "Or here."

Her fingers settled in his silky black locks. "Right there."

He gave her one, long luscious lick, and just like that, she soared the heights into orgasm.

Tāwera placed a delicate kiss on top of her still pulsing nub before rising to draw her into his arms. He was big and muscular and warm. All hers.

"Did that help with the lingering aches?" she asked, smiling at him.

"I still ache." His grin turned naughty as he fisted his renewed erection.

"So I see," she murmured. "We can fix that too, but seriously, do you have a problem all the time, or does it become worse during the full moon then ease?"

"My pain is worse during my moonlust, but with you here, I am whole. Healthy."

"Me too," Nyree murmured. "Rollover."

He stared at her quizzically and did as she ordered. Nyree straddled his hips and guided his cock to her entrance before bearing down. Her pace was unhurried as she sank onto his shaft.

"Nyree," Tāwera whispered, his eyes more golden in the privacy of his bedroom. "That is incredible."

"Wait, there's more," she said, and her grin felt lighthearted and happy. She rolled her hips before rising and sinking again. She rocked while watching Tāwera's handsome, tattooed face. His golden-brown gaze was intense, his enjoyment in doing this with her—making love—palpable, and his pleasure fed her own. Faster and faster, she went until their harsh breaths filled the room. Tāwera gripped her hips with his big hands, and his eyes narrowed.

"Nyree, yes," he whispered, driving his hips upward to meet each of her downward slides. Nyree stroked her clit, and Tāwera watched her with his intense gaze. "You are so beautiful."

"You're the beautiful one," she replied, shrugging aside his words.

"People..." He paused and gritted his teeth, his face a mask of masculine satisfaction as he lost control and gave in to his climax.

Nyree stroked her swollen nub and followed him a heartbeat later. She fell forward, boneless, and his muscular arms wrapped around her. Once again, it was like coming home.

"People what?" she asked as they cuddled in the aftermath, their pulses still racing. The thud of his heart comforted her, and she yawned, exhaustion catching up with her.

"When I walk down the street, either with Manu or our other friends or alone, people stare at me. My facial tattoos scare some. A few cross the road instead of walking past me."

"That's their problem, not yours," Nyree said fiercely. "I bet none of our tribe treat you in this way."

"No. Manu suggested we not tell any except our close friends about the curse and my origins. He said while he trusted most of his people, he didn't want anyone to slip and spread the truth by mistake."

"Understandable." Nyree played with a lock of his hair, the silky strand bringing familiarity and comfort. "Are you going to continue working with Manu and George Taniwha & Sons?"

"Yes, I enjoy the work and the variety, and it allows me to learn. I find I enjoy education. It's part of the reason I learned to read and write English when the missionaries came to our village. Will you live in my house with me?"

"Yes." She smiled because now that she was in his arms, it was such a simple decision. She'd forgotten how spending time with

Tāwera soothed her, and she found his curiosity and his quest for knowledge endlessly fascinating. "I, too, wish to support you and enjoy a future together." She pushed up on one elbow so she could see his face. "I have a confession. I missed you from the moment you left South Georgia with Manu. Once you left, my mind took me to dark places. I worried you'd find another woman who suited you better. Each day I told myself we were merely friends, and it was too soon for a relationship after Ari."

Tāwera's brows lifted. "You lied to yourself."

Nyree laughed, a wry, derisive sound that echoed within the room. "I did, and my jealousy grew in proportion. It was difficult to read your emails about everything you were doing and the people you were meeting."

"For the last time, Nyree. It is you whom I love. You make me laugh and smile and wish to get up each morning. And it is you who makes my heart beat faster, and my passion grows each time I see you. You are the woman I wish to stand at my side, and if you do not want the same, tell me now."

Nyree rolled on top of Tāwera and cupped his face in her hands.

"You've been honest with me and told me what was in your heart. I could do nothing less. In my roundabout way, I was trying to explain I was jealous because my feelings for you ran deep. I love you, Tāwera, and that is my last word on the matter."

Tāwera chuckled, his laugh full of joy and a touch of humor. "Then sleep, my love, because I will keep you busy in my bed later."

Nyree shifted onto her side, and Tāwera cuddled her from behind. She drifted off to sleep in Tāwera's arms with a smile curving her lips.

Her man. Her love. Their future.

CHAPTER 20

Wedding Joy

One year later

Emma sat beside Nyree in the lunchroom at George Taniwha & Sons.

"When are you and Tāwera getting married?"

Nyree paused, her forkful of salad hovering at mouth level. "He hasn't asked me."

"But it's obvious you adore each other. You've been living together for almost a year now."

Nyree shrugged. "It doesn't matter to me. Marriage, I mean. I have complete faith in Tāwera. He is the most honest and decent man I know apart from your husband and our other male friends,

268

of course."

"*Hmm.*" Emma picked up her coffee and took a sip.

"What?" Nyree asked.

"There is no reason you can't ask Tāwera to marry you. He might not realize you'd like a wedding ring."

"I never said that," Nyree protested.

"I saw your face when Hana announced her engagement."

"You saw nothing," Nyree contradicted. "Tāwera and I are as good as married. I'm happy for my sister, and I approve of her choice of husband."

"But what about kids?" Emma persisted.

"Newsflash. Marriage is unnecessary to have children."

But Emma's words got her thinking about babies. They've never discussed children in detail, just tossed the idea into their future, but Tāwera was great with kids, and they loved him in return.

The phone rang at the reception desk, and Nyree stood to answer the summons. The afternoon was busy with clients popping in to speak to their team of private investigators. Failed marriages, cheating, and divorces were a large part of their business and a handbrake on the idea of happy-ever-after.

Yet, she'd never been more content.

She and Tāwera hadn't discussed marriage or children recently since they were satisfied with the status quo.

Or were they?

Nyree thought hard during the bus journey home. Tāwera

treated her like a queen while she tried her best to do little things each day to surprise him and give him new experiences he'd never had because of his cursed past. Their relationship had never been a traditional one. It was more of a shared journey, their intimacy growing with each passing day.

Her mind drifted to marriage and children again, the possibility of a family pet, and suddenly, the answer became obvious.

She practically skipped from the bus stop to their home. Once there, she took steaks from the freezer and prepared vegetables. Next up was a special cake for dessert. Carrot, she decided, since it was Tāwera's favorite.

Once the meal was under control, she picked a few flowers from the garden and set the table. A bottle of champagne already sat in the fridge along with Tāwera's favorite cheeses. She chose a wedge of brie and a sharp cheddar and placed them on the counter to bring them to room temperature.

Satisfied she'd done everything to prepare, she focused on herself. After a quick shower, she dressed in her sexiest lingerie and a dress that was one of Tāwera's favorites. He never failed to compliment her when she wore it on an outing.

Tāwera arrived home while she was putting the last touches to her makeup.

"Honey, I'm home!" he roared from the entranceway.

Nyree grinned. He always did that, and the ritual always amused her. "I'm in the bedroom."

The front door shut, and firm footsteps heralded him, heading in her direction. He came to an abrupt standstill in the doorway. "Are we going somewhere tonight? Have I forgotten an outing?"

"No, we're having dinner at home. You take a shower, and I'll pour you a drink once I hear the water stop running. Go," she urged, excitement pulsing through her. "I'll get dinner underway too."

"Kiss first," Tāwera said. "I must kiss my beautiful lady."

Nyree walked into his arms willingly, her heart beating faster as he wrapped her in a firm hug. An instant later, his lips met hers, and he kissed her languidly, the contact gradually deepening to passion. When they parted, Tāwera glanced at the bed.

"Save that thought for later," she said, keeping her voice firm to remind herself she had a plan. "Shower then a drink and dinner."

Tāwera winked at her and dragged his T-shirt over his head. Amusement filled her at the way both of his eyes flickered shut for seconds before her gaze drifted lower. The sight of his broad chest never failed to thrill her, and she stared until she realized her man was doing his best to entice her into bed.

She raised her hands in surrender and backed up, her giggle broadening Tāwera's grin. "I'm pouring us a drink. Get that sexy body of yours into the shower." With a wink of her own aimed over her shoulder, she retreated to the kitchen.

When Tāwera emerged from the bathroom fifteen minutes later, she saw he'd dressed in nice clothes too. Perfect. She approached him with a drink in hand.

His brows rose as he accepted the glass. "Champagne?"

Nyree merely smiled and lifted her flute. "To us. To the future, and to love."

"A toast to us, the future and deep, sexy love," he said and took a sip of his drink. "Something smells delicious. I'm starving."

"I've cooked steak, jacket potatoes, green beans in a special tomato sauce. We have carrot cake for dessert."

Tāwera beamed. "My favorites."

"What can I say? I enjoy pleasing you." She lifted her glass and smiled at him over the fluted rim.

During their meal, they discussed their days and their plans for the near future.

"Manu mentioned I have holidays accrued. I want to go on a plane. Where can we go?"

"We can fly to a place in New Zealand or farther afield. Perhaps somewhere in the Pacific. One of the islands or Australia." No! She had the perfect place in mind and made a plan to arrange holiday time for both of them.

"That was tasty." Tāwera patted his stomach, his body still robust and in perfect condition because of the training he did with Manu and the others.

"I think we'll have dessert in the lounge. Why don't you choose some music while I grab our cake?"

When she arrived with the carrot cake, a slow waltz played.

"Will you dance with me, my sweet Nyree?"

Her heart melting, she set the plates on the coffee table and slipped into his arms. They slow danced to three songs, content in each other's arms. At the end of the third song, Nyree leaned back. She studied his familiar face, and her heart clenched with the wealth of love that filled her. This man was her everything.

"Tāwera, I have a question for you."

"Yes?"

"Will you marry me?" Nyree had wondered if she might stutter her way through the question, but her words were strong and even. She met Tāwera's golden-brown gaze and waited for his response.

The pause grew longer, and she worried she'd miscalculated or got things wrong.

His somber expression transformed without haste. His eyes picked up a glow to match his excited smile.

"Yes, I would be honored to marry you," he said in a husky voice. "I thought it was the man's job to ask for a woman's hand in marriage?"

"That is the traditional way," she agreed. "But nothing about our relationship has been normal. Not the way we met, nor the behavior of our taniwha."

"That's true," Tāwera agreed. "My dragon continues to prefer sex rather than flying."

"You truly want to marry me?"

"I want you as my legal wife. Manu explained it to me. We live and act like a couple, which means you are my wife in the eyes of the law."

"While that's true, I yearn for tradition. I'd like to see a ring on your finger and one on mine. I would like to have a child with you. Soon."

"Yes." Tāwera held her. They stood close enough for her to feel his racing heart. "Yes," he repeated, and she saw the emotion in him.

"I have a suggestion of where we should get married."

"I am all ears," he said and lifted one hand to tug an earlobe.

Nyree chuckled. Tāwera never failed to amuse her with his adoption of the common sayings. "We'll fly to Samoa and get married there. We can invite our friends and family to come with us. This way, you'll get to use your passport and fly in a plane."

"That is an excellent idea," Tāwera said. "You are clever. We will have a memorable wedding day."

"We will," she agreed. "Who would you like to invite?"

They made a list while they ate their carrot cake.

"Tomorrow, we will start the arrangements," Nyree said.

"I wish to help every step of the way. Show me how to do everything."

Six weeks later, they boarded a plane for Samoa.

"I am so excited," Tāwera said.

"Me too," Nyree agreed.

Manu and Jessalyn, Emma and Jack, Hone and Cassie, and Nyree's mother and Hana and her fiancé boarded the flight with them.

The flight was uneventful, and Tāwera appeared to enjoy every moment. Nyree showed him how to collect their bags and to fill out the immigration forms.

"You are very patient," Tāwera said.

"I enjoy seeing the world from your eyes," Nyree countered. "You throw yourself into every situation. You're enthusiastic, and it's a joy to see your reactions to things I think are normal. Most of us take our modern society for granted. You make us view our lives differently."

"Everyone is tolerant with me," Tāwera countered. "But I take pleasure in learning new things."

They checked into the hotel, and Nyree had fun showing Tāwera around the resort. She revealed where the ceremony would take place and told him what to expect, then they spent the afternoon and evening swimming, eating, and enjoying time with their friends.

The next morning, Nyree woke in Tāwera's arms. Their lazy kisses turned to passion as they made love.

"I will be happy if I wake this way each day—with you in my

arms," Tāwera said.

"Yes," Nyree agreed with a lazy stretch. "Tomorrow morning, we will wear each other's rings."

"I love the life we have built together. Each day is better, and my lady grows more beautiful."

"Tāwera," Nyree whispered. "You make me so happy. You will make a wonderful husband and father."

"And you will make an excellent mother, and we have plenty of people to look after our children should we decide we wish to have special time alone."

Nyree smiled against his broad chest and pulled away a fraction to see his face. "About that special time alone," she said. "That might end sooner than we'd planned."

"What?" Tāwera sent her a blank look.

"I'm fairly certain I'm pregnant."

Tāwera's eyes grew wide and round. "Really? So soon?"

"Yes."

A beam broke out on his face. "That's wonderful. I can't think of a better wedding present."

Nyree returned his smile, joy in her heart. "Me neither."

"Let's celebrate," he said, and he kissed her gently.

The minutes grew to hours, interrupted only by room service with the breakfast they'd ordered the previous night. They lazed and slept and made love again.

A thump woke them, followed by a feminine holler. Nyree

recognized Emma's shout instantly.

"What time is it?"

"One o'clock," Tāwera replied after glancing at his watch.

"Our wedding is in an hour." Nyree leaped off the bed, her gaze going to the locked door on which her friend was banging with enthusiasm.

"We know you're in there," Jessalyn shouted. "Tāwera, you need to join the boys in our room and get dressed while we have our turn with the bride."

"Is this an important tradition?" Tāwera asked.

Nyree smiled. "Yes."

Tāwera climbed out of bed and pulled on underwear. "I'll get the door and tell them you're in the shower. I can shower at Manu's place."

"Thank you." Nyree gave him a quick kiss. "Baby Daddy," she whispered before fleeing.

Manu grabbed a pair of shorts and donned them, too, before answering the door. "Nyree is in the shower," he said before any of the three women could say a word. "I'll grab my wedding clothes and leave you to it."

"We thought we'd see you at breakfast," Jessalyn said.

"No, we ordered room service last night. We had things to discuss."

"Like what?" Emma demanded.

"Can I tell the men about your being pregnant? Are you certain?"

he asked Nyree through their mind link.

"I am almost positive. My mother told me you can sense when you're with child. It's a quirk of the taniwha genes," Nyree replied. *"I thought I would tell the women. You may tell the men."*

"I'll see you later, Nyree."

"You will." Her tender voice echoed through Tāwera's mind, bringing warmth to his chest.

Happiness filled his heart to overflowing, and his mouth ached from smiling so wide. Rāwiri might have cursed him, but to Tāwera's mind, his life had changed in the best way. He'd won, and Rāwiri had lost.

He knocked on Manu's door, and it flew open to reveal his friends.

"They kicked me out. I'll have to shower and dress here," Tāwera explained.

"What have you been doing? We haven't seen you all morning." Hone searched Tāwera's face and held up his hand in a stop motion. "Wait, don't tell us. I have a fair idea of what you've been doing."

"We're having a baby," Tāwera said and grinned widely.

"Congratulations," Manu said, slapping him over the back.

"I must get ready for the wedding." The last thing Tāwera wanted was to arrive late.

An hour later, he waited with his friends for the women to appear.

Everyone who mattered to him and Nyree was here for this important day.

"We're ready," Nyree's sweet voice rippled through his mind, and he straightened.

"They're on their way." Tāwera turned to watch for Nyree's arrival.

His first glimpse of her stole his breath. She wore a long white dress that clung to her supple form. Her black hair rippled down over her bare shoulders, and her smile was bright and wide and full of the same excitement that filled him. When she had almost reached him, he crossed the distance between them and held out his hand to her.

She placed her hand in his, he curled their fingers together, and everything in his world was right. Nyree was here. Her mother and sister were here and safe. His friends and workmates.

"I love you, Nyree," he said in a loud voice that made the women sigh.

"I love you too, Tāwera. Let's get married."

So they moved to stand in front of the marriage celebrant and said their vows before their friends. The women sighed again when the celebrant announced them, man and wife, while the men cheered. Then they celebrated with food and music, and there was no one happier than Tāwera. He had a beautiful wife and a child on the way.

He drew his new wife into his arms, and they danced. Nyree

smiled up at him, and he pulled her closer.

"I have never been so happy."

"Me neither," Nyree said, and they danced under the moonlight and celebrated with their friends, ready to embrace their future.

Want a peek at Nyree's Photo Journal?

Not quite ready to let Tāwera and Nyree go? Me neither. Subscribe to my newsletter (https://shelleymunro.com/newsletter/) and receive a copy of Nyree's Photo Journal. See some of the places she and Tāwera visited. I also wrote a scene from the villain's point of view that I decided not to include in the final version of **Snow Moon Dragon**. Grab a copy of that scene too.

Glossary

Kororāreka – Russell, which is a Northland town.

Rāwiri – a Christian name that translates to David.

Pūriri – a New Zealand native tree with glossy, dark green leaves and pink to red flowers, which attract the birds.

Whare – house or dwelling.

Pā – a fortified village.

Whānau – extended family.

Tāwera – Morning star.

Aroha – Love.

Pākehā – A New Zealander of European descent.

Hongi – a traditional greeting where noses are pressed together.

Mana – a person's prestige or influence. Their status.

Taniwha – a dragon from Māori mythology. Some—water dragons—live in lakes, rivers or the sea. Legend says a taniwha lives at every bend of a river. Other taniwha are cave dwellers and have the ability to fly. Some are benevolent while others are mischievous tricksters or true villains.

Tohunga tā moko – An expert in tattooing.

Pōhutukawa – New Zealand tree that bears scarlet flowers at Christmastime.

Hone – Māori for John, and a very common Christian name.

Manu – Māori, meaning man of the birds or a person held in high esteem.

Wirihana – Name. Wilson.

Utu – To repay or avenge.

Aotearoa – Māori name for New Zealand (Land of the Long White Cloud)

Piupiu – a garment made of flax. It also means to move, swing or sway, which is what the dried flax does when a piupiu is worn.

Haka – a ceremonial dance. Often associated with war to stir passion for the coming battle. If you're a rugby fan, you'll see the haka performed by the All Blacks before each international game. Facial features can be contorted and tongue poked out as part of the rhythmic performance.

Tohunga – an expert in their chosen field.

Wāka – a canoe.

Hāngī – an earth oven where the food is steamed in the ground. Heated rocks are used to produce the heat for cooking.

Kūmara – sweet potato.

Mere – a flat club, often made from greenstone.

Taiaha – a wooden staff used as a weapon. These days used in ceremonial greetings.

Kai – food.

Pīwakawaka – a small insect-eating bird with a tail that resembles a fan.

Waiata – a song.

Ure – Cock

Moko – traditional tattoos on the face.

Tamariki - children

Kahurangi – Māori, meaning sky blue or precious.

About Shelley

USA Today bestselling author Shelley Munro lives in Auckland, the City of Sails, with her husband and a cheeky Jack Russell/mystery breed dog.

Typical New Zealanders, Shelley and her husband left home for their big OE soon after they married (translation of New Zealand speak - big overseas experience). A twelve-month-long adventure lengthened to six years of roaming the world. Enduring memories include being almost sat on by a mountain gorilla in Rwanda, lazing on white sandy beaches in India, whale watching in Alaska, searching for leprechauns in Ireland, and dealing with ghosts in an English pub.

While travel is still a big attraction, these days Shelley is most likely found in front of her computer following another love - that of writing stories of contemporary and paranormal romance and adventure. Other interests include watching rugby (strictly for research purposes), cycling, playing croquet and the ukelele, and curling up with an enjoyable book.

Visit Shelley at her Website

https://shelleymunro.com

Join Shelley's Newsletter

https://shelleymunro.com/newsletter

Also By Shelley

My Plan B
My Cat Nap
My Romantic Tangle
My Blue Lady
My Twin Trouble
My Precious Gift

Middlemarch Gathering
My Highland Mate
My Highland Fling
My Elusive Mate
My Valiant Princess
My Highland Wedding
My Highland Billionaire